SAILING AGAINST THE TIDE

Jeanne Baret, the First Woman
to Circumnavigate the Globe

Cindy Burkart Maynard

HISTORIUM PRESS U.S.A.

First Edition 2025

Standard Images by Shutterstock & Public Domain

Main cover image copyrighted and protected © Cindy Burkart Maynard

Cover designed by White Rabbit Arts

Visit Cindy Burkart Maynard's website at

www.cindyburkartmaynard.com

Paperback ISBN: 978-1-964700-65-6

E-Book ISBN: 978-1-964700-66-3

Historium Press, a subsidiary of

The Historical Fiction Company

2025

Table of Contents

CHAPTER ONE

I, JEANNE
LA COMELLE, France - SPRING 1746

I cannot remember my mother. I was an infant when she died. But when I close my eyes, I hear her voice like the breath of angels whispering me to sleep.

> *Lullay, lullay, my little child,*
> *Sleep and be now still;*
> *If thou be a little child,*
> *Yet may thou have thy will.*

My reverie dissipates when I hear Father's voice from across the dinner table recapturing me from my reverie. "Tomorrow, I need all three of you working in the fields. The days are getting longer, and the time for rest is growing short. If we want to eat next winter, we must tend our fields." Father chides. He is old, weathered by wind and work, bent from a lifetime hunched over the plough and hoe, laboring on the small plot of land we rented from the owner, Seigneur Girard. "Pierre, you are strong enough now to plough. And Marie, you follow him with the hoe. Make nice, even furrows. You have skill at that task." He nods, indicating that the conversation is finished.

Turning to me he says "Jeanne, run outside, and put the hens in the coop. I heard a wolf howl last night, and we need to keep our chickens safe. Tomorrow, it is your job to look after them. Chase off any stray dogs, with a stick." He bends to kiss the top of my head.

It's a big job for a six-year-old, but if Father thinks I can do it, I will do my best. I've been collecting eggs since I was five, and the chickens all know me. I love the way they sing to me when they see me coming. I scatter a few handfuls of breadcrumbs as they burble happily. I know I shouldn't because one day soon Father will chop their skinny heads off with an ax, but I have given them names. I slip into their yard and six fat, fluffy hens flock to me. Babou, Babette, Mon chou, Loulou, Lapin, and Poule push each other to get the best spot. Babette is the bossy one, and despite trying to feed them all equally, she always gets more than her share. In the evening, they ascend the steps to their coop, always in the same order and arrange themselves, each in her own little nest. I haul up the ladder and make sure the door is closed tight. "Sleep safely my girls."

Our home is humble indeed, made of wattle and daub, with a low thatched roof, hardly any more luxurious than the hen house. A single room serves for living, sleeping, cooking, and eating. Our small family - Father, sister Marie, brother Pierre, and I – share the work to ensure we have food to eat and a place to lay our heads. But we share more than our daily bread. We share the love only a family can give. I feel as secure and carefree as my little flock.

I wrapped myself in a coarse woolen blanket and curled up in a corner of the hut with my sister, Marie. She is three years older than I and remembers more about Mother than I do. She drapes her arm over my shoulder and curls her body behind mine to keep us both warm. I can smell the scents of the countryside, clover, cut grass, compost and manure, on her well-worn dress.

Mother died when I was a newborn, and my sister was only three. Phillipe was six, and he at least could be of some use to Father, so he spent his days at Father's side. One of the village ladies came in to prepare our meals and care for Marie and me. We called her Auntie Juliette. She was widowed long ago and supported herself as the village herb woman and as our nanny. Our predicament, having lost our mother to the childbed, was not unusual. Until a widower man found another wife, he sought the services of women like Juliette, herself a widow and too old to remarry. As soon as we were old enough to walk through high grass without falling, we followed Auntie Juliette to glean food from the hills around the village. Marie and I tripped along behind Auntie Juliette and absorbed her store of knowledge about wild plants as a sponge absorbs water. Auntie taught us how to scour the countryside for herbs, berries, small fruits, and nuts that fell from the gnarled trees. By the time I was nine years old, I was strong and curious enough to have learned all Juliette could teach us, yet I was voracious for more knowledge. Whenever we were not needed in the fields, we roamed the hills and forests, hunting for fruit, herbs, and medicinal plants. The healing plants fascinated me most of all.

"Every plant that our Lord put on this earth has a use," she opined. "Every ailment of the body has a treatment. We will all die, but we herb women can at least allay suffering."

I held her teachings in my heart. I would be proud to grow up to be an herb woman just like Juliette.

Pierre's lot was more difficult than Marie's and mine. When he was only nine years old, he had already started clawing at the earth with a hoe Father had shortened for him. By the time he was twelve he was doing a man's work in the fields at Father's side. At about that time Pierre started sprouting hair from his chin and lip, he grew itchy and irritable, complaining about the amount of work expected of him. Father did not tolerate his complaints. Though he did not strike Pierre, he clapped his staff against the table and shouted.

"How do you expect us to live if we don't work? You realize, don't you, that this hut belongs to the Seigneur and the moment we do not produce an acceptable crop for him, he has the right to evict us. Then how will we live?"

Pierre shuffled his feet, grumbling as he looked at the ground. An expression of hopelessness dragged down the corners of his mouth.

"Think of someone other than yourself for once. You are the eldest, and as I get older you must take up my responsibilities, feeding these girls until they are old enough to find husbands." He pointed directly at Marie and me as if we had misbehaved. I clung to her skirts baffled by Father's outburst. He was usually even-tempered, but on this day, he did not try to disguise his displeasure. "Now go. Harness the oxen unless you wish to pull the plough yourself."

Though I cannot name the feeling that shot through me. I understood for the first time that our lives here in our simple hut may not last forever. Roaming the hills with my sister and Auntie Juliette was my principal pleasure, but tending the fields for the Seigneur was everyone's responsibility. No one was exempt from laboring in the fields, neither men nor women, boys nor girls.

CHAPTER TWO

PLANTING NEW SEEDS
LA COMELLE to TOULON-SUR-ARROUX 1756

A bitter and unforgiving winter followed a dry fruitless summer. In spring, when the unusually heavy snow melted, fields and forests erupted in ambitious growth. Plants, both wild and farmed, grew uncommonly tall and robust. Then in midsummer, the rain ceased, and the promising greenery of spring wilted then dried, leaving the landscape pocked with tall dead stems and shriveled flowers and fruit. The crops languished under the sallow sun, as dry and brittle as cinders. Everyone and everything in La Comelle was hungry. Farm horses' heads drooped to the ground, refusing to pull their ploughs across the hardened earth. No amount of flogging, whistling, pushing or pulling could get them to move.

Father began to droop too. I knew he was getting older, and would naturally lose his youthful vigor, but this was more than simple weariness. Marie married two years ago, and now, with a baby balanced on her hip, she spent her days making a home for her husband, Antoinne, and her child. In hopes of earning hard cash Pierre slipped the noose and moved to a farm three hours' walk from our hut, far enough away to be of no help at home. They visited infrequently. It was not that they didn't want to see Father and me, they just didn't have time for the long walk to our hut.

Now only Father and I labored in the fields. When I looked up from my hoe I saw a broken man, old beyond his years. The final blow came in late summer when I was sixteen. One day, as we toiled in the open field, a sudden deluge poured down on us. We slipped and staggered as we struggled through slippery, clinging mud trying to make our way home. I threw Father's arm across my shoulders and practically dragged him through the doorway. I laid him on his woolen blanket, now worn thin, and warmed the weak stew I made the day before, but he was too exhausted to sip the broth I spooned to his lips. He slept through the night and most of the following day. When he woke, his cough was violent and painful. Over the next several weeks he worsened, and soon yellow mucous dribbled from his mouth with each bout of coughing. I tugged him into a sitting position leaning him against my chest. He shivered violently and his lips became unnaturally blue. I wrapped his thin blanket around both of us attempting to warm him with my own body heat. Sweat coursed down his back, his skin hot to the touch, and his breath came in quick gasps. I wracked my brain, summoning up the cures I had learned from Auntie Juliette.

"Here Father, take a sip of this," I coaxed. He grumbled and shook his head, dodging the proffered cup. "Come, take it. It will help. It's a simple tea made with feverfew, licorice root and honey."

I leaned my ear near to his lips to hear his raspy voice. "All I want is to sleep without waking. I'm done. I hope God does not curse me by allowing me to see tomorrow's dawn." Father turned his head to the wall and shivered.

"No Father, I still need you," I whined. "Together we will bring in this year's crop and next year will be better."

His eyes found mine. I could see clouds forming in them as he drifted further and further away. "You are my good and faithful daughter. I know you will do well in this world. I haven't given you much, but I've blessed you with the strength of a horse and the fortitude of an unyielding oak."

"I am proud to be just like you, Father," my voice began to quaver. "You have been my rock."

"Your other traits are blessings from God," his voice barely audible. "Your steadfast loyalty, your determination, your stoic strength in the face of hardship. You will find your way."

He had never spoken to me like this. He was a hard-working, down-to-earth farmer of very few words. Personal conversations never interrupted the practicalities of everyday life, and this one terrified me. I rocked him through the night, until finally I laid him down and crumpled on the blanket beside him. God granted his wish, and that night he passed into the next world. By morning he had become cool and rigid. What would I do without him?

* * *

I knew I could do nothing to save our farm without the strong back of a man. I was adrift. At fifteen I was of marriageable age, but I had no prospects. I knew I could not manage the farm by myself and besides, Seigneur Claude would never allow a single woman to continue to work and live alone in the hut. He would certainly find a strong, steady man to take Father's place. Apart from farming, I had no skills other than those Juliette had taught me.

The funeral was as simple as Father's life had been. After the funeral, my sister Marie, took my hand and led me from the church. "You will come home with me," she said matter-of-factly.

"But you live in Toulon-sur-Arroux and I have always lived in La Comelle."

"That's right. And it will be good for you to leave this little village behind with all its bad memories. You can help with my household duties and help take care of the baby. When time allows, you and I can go out herb hunting." She knew the prospect of roaming the hills searching for herbs would please me.

I brightened. "Perhaps I can sell herbs to the townspeople. That would bring in a little extra income, wouldn't it?"

"We'll see," she said. "One step at a time. For now, you will come live with us."

Though I loved my sister, she and I were as similar as water and wax. Marie was only three years older than I, but at eighteen she was in every way a grown woman. She was tall, stately and lean, with an open visage that showed she was a friend to all, and a demeanor both women and men found attractive. She was content in her domestic duties and well-liked by the townspeople. She was always the first woman to come to a neighbor's aid when needed.

When I walked through the door of her house, the insistent wails of her one-year-old son, Roman, greeted us. "Mama, Mama," he hollered.

"You take him," her husband, Antoinne said, handing the baby over the Marie. "I need to get back to the barn to muck the stalls and feed the horses."

"Are you overlooking something?" Marie smiled, nodding in my direction.

"Oh, it's you, Jeanne. I'm sorry about the death of your father," he called over his shoulder as he headed for the door.

"Wait!" she called. "Now that Father has died, Jeanne's hut will revert to the Seigneur, and she will have nowhere to stay. So, I invited her into our home."

Antoinne turned to face me as he paused a moment to consider this. "Well, we may be a little cramped for space, but you are welcome here." He did not smile about the prospect of having another mouth to feed, but he didn't oppose Marie's wishes.

"Yes, we might be a bit cramped," Marie smiled. She winked at Antoine and gave him a saucy smile. He stopped and planted his hands on his hips and looked at her with suspicion.

"What do you mean?"

"In about six months' time, we will have another little one to bless our marriage."

"Heaven help us!" Antoinne rolled his eyes. He came to Marie's side, nuzzled her neck, and gave her a kiss full on the mouth. I turned away in shock. I'd never seen such a thing.

"Go now! You are embarrassing our new family member." Marie smiled coquettishly and pushed him away.

So began the baby years. In the five years I was with them, Marie and Antoinne produced three more children for me to dote on and love. It was as close to family bliss as I ever got. As generous as they were, I knew they were stretching to feed so many hungry mouths. If I was going to contribute to my sister's growing family, I must earn my keep doing the only thing I knew - hunting herbs. I took to the hills, fields and forests single-mindedly gleaning every curative or tasty herb I could find. I peddled them from my basket directly to our friends and neighbors and walked to the weekly market. I was now officially the herb lady.

CHAPTER THREE

THE BOTANIST AND THE PEASANT
1760

Hunger pangs shot through me as I bent over, searching the hillside for useful plants. A glance skyward told me it was nearly midday. Hours had passed since my breakfast of black bread and raspberry leaf tea. Hungry or not, I needed to hunt the herbs my neighbors would pay for - chamomile to soothe a neighbor's sleeplessness, yarrow to make a compress for the inflamed cut on another's arm, witch hazel for a poultice to apply to a man's swollen legs.

Within another eighteen months Marie was pregnant again. She and her husband were exceptionally generous allowing me to live with them since Father's death, but the house was crowded with children. And though she was always kind, regardless how harried she was, I felt like just another burden she must carry. I contributed what labor I could to the household, tending a garden plot, and selling my herbs, but I but I was still another burden for them to carry.

These concerns weighed on me as I toiled up the hillside, combing field and forest for useful plants. I kept one eye out for edible plants to ease my family's hunger. Sometimes I found leeks, rose hips, or, if I was very lucky, a stand of late-season wild asparagus. With the other eye, I scanned the hillside for seasonings for the pot or curatives to ease common maladies.

My mind wandered back to the winters when I was still living with Father and too young to work in the fields. Father was indulgent with me, the youngest, and encouraged me to attend the lessons taught by the parish priest, Father Luc. Dim light filtered into the ancient church through one small circular window, not strong enough to dry the perpetually damp stone walls. Father Luc, an elven man who always wore a soft, round chapel cap, welcomed the few nearby children whose parents dismissed them from chores when the fields lay fallow in winter. I didn't need much encouragement, as the classroom lessons satisfied my deep curiosity and hunger for knowledge. I remember the day when Father Luc shivered with excitement as he made an announcement to the six shivering children in the front pew.

"I have a surprise! I have a gift for you." Smiling broadly, he distributed his gift as ceremoniously as holy communion. Father Luc gave each of us a small notepad and rounded stick into which a graphite stick was inserted. "This is called a pencil. It is much easier to use than a quill pen and inkpot and doesn't require a slate board as chalk does. You will use these implements to write down those lessons you cannot commit to memory."

He surveyed our puzzled faces. "Go ahead! Write your name on the paper."

We bent to the task and soon happy smiles lit up our dirty faces. We got only one pencil and to me it was a sacred object, a relic like the bone of a saint at a shrine. I made a habit of writing what I saw when foraging for useful plants. I recorded when each plant matured each year, and where they liked to grow. I noted plants growing out of season, or in other unusual places, and best of all those plants I had never seen before.

I spent as much time as I could outdoors searching for plants. One day in early spring, when mother nature's generous gifts were least abundant, hunger overtook me, and I dropped heavily onto the grassy hillside to eat lunch. I was dizzy, my breathing was labored, and my heartbeat reverberated in my ears. I sipped water from my gourd hoping it would steady me. From my familiar perch on the hillside, I spotted a man struggling up the steep slope with a large wicker basket slung over his back. From a distance he resembled a huge beetle. At first, I thought my hunger was creating apparitions, but as he came closer, the beetle-man image resolved into the form of an ordinary man bending down, intent on plucking plants from the earth and depositing them into the basket strapped to his back. He was in his middle years, dressed in a long, linen shirt that hung loosely about his torso, a red waistcoat flapping open, fine leather boots, long stockings, and a wide-brimmed hat. Though he was disheveled, these were the clothes of a prosperous gentleman. Clearly, he was no peasant.

He could certainly afford to buy food, I thought, so what was he doing out here hunting plants? Judging from his awkward, uneven gait and his obvious struggle to climb uphill, I guessed he was new to the art of foraging and therefore clumsily inept. I heaved my reluctant body up and went about my work, putting the puzzling man out of my thoughts. I had much to accomplish if I was going to fill my customers' orders, and I had no time for idle curiosity.

Later in the day, I inched my way back down the hill combing through whatever plants I might had missed along the way. As surefooted as the sheep that roamed the hills, and as familiar with the landscape as the plovers stalking through the grass, I kept my eyes focused downward, mentally cataloging every plant and estimating when each would reach its peak for harvesting. Absorbed as I was in my task, I did not look up again until a man's shoes filled my field of vision. I jolted to a halt. Slowly my eyes traveled up his stockinged legs, to his linen shirt, and the unbuttoned red waistcoat. When my gaze reached his face, I stood. I was almost nose to nose with the turtle-backed man.

"Mon Dieu!" I gasped, so startled I dropped my basket, my hard-won harvest tumbling to the ground.

"I'm so sorry. I didn't mean to startle you." The man's voice was low and velvety smooth with a highly refined Parisian accent. "Here, let me help you with those." He bent down, and together we returned the herbs to my basket. We stood up in unison and found ourselves less than an arm's length apart. The man eyed me intently, assessing me as if I was a museum artifact. I was suddenly aware of how bedraggled I must appear to him. I tucked stray whisps of my mousey brown hair into my head scarf and brushed the day's detritus from my skirts. Filled with suspicion, I eyed him warily. I was too tired to summon the deference befitting a man of his station. In my estimation, he was an outsider who did not belong here on *my* hillside, why should I demurely shrink from his gaze.

In me, he must have seen a species of woman far removed from the well-bred young demoiselles who no doubt circulated in his milieu. He saw a very common woman, underweight but with the strong, well-muscled arms of a farmer - a woman, no longer a girl, whose first blush of womanhood had come and gone, neither young nor old, neither beautiful nor ugly. I was perfectly ordinary, yet he could not take his eyes off me. I was too tired to care what he thought. I stood straight and maintained my composure.

"You have quite a collection of plants there," he said. "Do you gather herbs on these hills often?" He dove into the conversation without so much as asking my name or introducing himself.

"Yes," I said curtly, with no intention of elaborating.

"Are you knowledgeable about the plants in this area?"

"Yes. I have been collecting herbs here since I was old enough to follow the adults into the countryside." The arrogance of his manner galled me. Apparently, he thought he was entitled to pry.

"What will you do with the herbs you have gathered?" he asked.

"I sell them in the village. People come to me to request my help treating their ailments." I paused, my eyes drilling into his. "And why are you asking me all these questions? I might as well ask you the same. What are you doing here? You are certainly not a local. I have never seen you here before." I abruptly turned to go. "I have no time for pointless conversation. I have work to do." Though I tried to display a haughty façade, I reeled with light-headedness born of hunger as I turned to walk away.

"Before you go," he called after me, "I have one more question. I am looking for a knowledgeable herb woman to help me expand my plant collection." I stopped walking but did not answer. "I can pay you for your assistance."

I turned slowly back toward him. This time I looked past his wardrobe and into his eyes. He was older than I, without the leering eyes or teasing tone of men looking to me for an evening's entertainment, and not dismissively like men of a higher class. Though not tall, he had a sturdy, broad-shouldered physique and his soft, pale hands revealed a life unused to physical labor. He piqued my curiosity. He appeared to be in good health, but a pronounced limp betrayed a serious injury.

"What happened to your leg?" I challenged him.

He was taken aback; his eyes widened then crinkled at the corners, vaguely amused, not knowing quite what to make of my directness. "I was bitten by a dog. The bite never fully healed, and it flares up from time to time."

As if not wanting me to think him pitiable, he drew himself up to his full height, threw his shoulders back and puffed out his chest. "I am a botanist. I collect plants for my extensive herbarium." He raised his chin. "I am a friend of Carl Linnaeus the most well-respected taxonomist in the country, perhaps the world. He is creating the most revolutionary system for classifying plants ever devised." He watched me carefully, waiting for my reaction.

I listened intently but betrayed no emotion.

"He chose me to be his assistant." He added as if mentioning this Linnaeus person gave him more importance.

The name meant nothing to me, but I sensed from the reverence with which he spoke it, that he was well respected among botanists. I was unimpressed by my new acquaintance's purported herbarium, but the prospect of earning actual coin transcended my feigned indifference.

"All right. I will help you for one day," I relented, "but I will not work for free. I will meet you here tomorrow at midmorning. After tomorrow, if I agree to help you further, I will expect suitable compensation. Now I must return to my work. If I do not deliver these remedies to my customers, they will not pay me." I paused, then added, "Since you did not bother to ask my name, I will tell you. My name is Jeanne Baret. And yours?"

"I am Philibert Commerson, medical doctor, botanist, and professor." I blinked and involuntarily dipped my chin slightly acknowledging his introduction. I hoped he was not as arrogant as he sounded.

"Hmmm," I said, looking him over from top to toe once more. "Tomorrow then."

That evening when I returned to my sister's home, I could barely summon the strength to rekindle the fire in the hearth as I usually did in the evening. My sister's home with all its noisy chaos of children was my island of security, crowded, but safe and welcoming. Commerson would no doubt be returning to a well-appointed country estate warmed by fireplaces in every room. He would not be wondering, as I did, if tomorrow he would have food to eat. I could not stop thinking of this man, Philibert Commerson. Despite my fatigue I slept fitfully that night.

Often, my customers paid me with bread, eggs, and garden vegetables. It had been a productive day, so I had been paid well, and the family went to bed with full stomachs. Tomorrow my routine would be unusual; I would not roam the hills alone. I would spend the day with Philibert Commerson. Despite my intention to remain dispassionate about the meeting, a tingle of anticipation crept up my spine.

The next morning, the sun rose gently, painting the underside of the wispy clouds a dusky rose, and tinting the fields and forests a muted, tawny yellow. The colors were soft and subtle, suggesting uncertain weather, but whatever the weather, the day promised to be exceptional. When mid-morning arrived, I stood alone on the hillside, expectant, and unsure of what I was getting into. I had committed only one day to Commerson, and if I did not approve of him, I could go on as before. I slipped my hand into the pocket of my skirt, my fingers stroking the notebook I had kept since I was a child learning to write. Other herb women had a wealth of knowledge passed down to them by their mothers, but I had my notebook. Since I first learned to write I had made notes of all the plants I found and where and when I had seen them. Year by year my notebook accumulated a treasure of local knowledge, carefully collected and documented.

I stood stoically as I watched Philibert toiling up the hill with his uneven gait. He winced with every step. I was surprised when a hint of sympathy warmed my heart. Why should I feel compassion for this aristocrat? He was just an educated name-dropper, thinking he could use me as a tool to advance his career.

No doubt I could help him, but I must not get ahead of myself. I would judge him by his behavior, not by his privilege, education, or connections. He had a high opinion of himself, perhaps rightly so, and today I would discover whether it was warranted or not.

Philibert waved his hat in the air when he spotted me. "Good morning!" he called. "A lovely day for botanizing." He grinned like a schoolboy on the last day of school.

"I have so many questions to ask," he dove into the conversation still panting from the climb. "Please, let us sit down for a moment so I can catch my breath and then we'll start over. Let me begin by re-introducing myself. I apologize if I gave you a poor impression upon our first meeting. As I said, I am a botanist, dedicated to investigating the relationships between plant families. My botanical studies have been mostly confined to the botanical gardens at the University of Montpellier where I studied medicine, and in Châtillon-les-Dombes, the town of my birth. I have established an extensive herbarium on my property, and I'm keen to increase my plant collections. I would value your help showing me the plants growing here in their wild, natural setting and sharing your knowledge." He smiled sheepishly. "I don't take your familiarity with herbs for granted, and for that reason, I am prepared to pay you a fair wage."

I looked at him steadily but made no comment. I could tell my stare unnerved him. I could almost feel his skin prickle as if lightning were about to strike.

I nodded. "Well then, let us begin," a sly half-smile teased the corners of my mouth. "What do you see here?" I swept my arm across the lush panorama of meadows, fields, and woods. Philibert was nonplussed; he expected to receive information, not to be quizzed by a peasant woman.

He sighed and tried not to roll his eyes. "It is a hillside with open fields and an abundance of potentially useful native plants."

"Yes, that's correct as far as it goes. But look again," I instructed. "To the left, over there, the hill drops off over an outcropping of rocks. At the bottom of the little cliff is a seep that creates a shallow marshy area. It supports an assortment of water-loving plants - water clover, flag irises and the like. And to the right, the grassy hillside ends at the margin of the woodland. The woodland belongs to the Seigneur, so we cannot forage there, but along the edge, where the meadow merges into the woodlot, there is a fascinating blending of two plant communities. I used to come here with my sister Marie and Juliette, my caretaker, when I was young. My favorite game was to commit to memory every plant that grew in each habitat, its uses, and the best season for harvesting it."

That caught his attention, and he sat up straighter. If he had been a dog, his ears would have been upright and on full alert, as if he had smelled a rabbit and was ready to chase it.

"You used to come here as a child? Did your mother come with you? Where is she now?" Involuntarily my face drooped, and I scanned the ground. Philibert immediately regretted his words. He realized it had been an inappropriately personal question and clearly elicited painful memories.

"She died." I said, swallowing hard, struggling not to betray my emotions. A shadow passed over my eyes. "She died only a few weeks after my birth. My father died and now I live with my sister's family." Now it was my turn to feel embarrassed. Despite my resolve to remain aloof, I had already revealed details far too personal to share with a total stranger. I sounded like a forlorn orphan.

"I am sorry to hear that." His tone revealed his genuine sympathy. "So, you earn your living selling herbs then?"

I guffawed in a rather unladylike manner. "Yes, I sell herbs hoping to earn my keep in my sister's household, but it hardly brings in enough to live on. I also help care for her family, do whatever household chores are called for, and tend the kitchen garden."

Philibert did not know how to respond. Surely, he had always been financially secure, and certainly never spared a moment's concern about the lives of the lower classes. My people worked as peasants and lived as peasants. We were not starving but we made only enough to keep us out of hunger's clutches."

His face was full of empathy, but he had no words with which to respond, so he straightened and resumed his professional demeanor. "We should begin," he said.

I was relieved to steer away from our overly personal conversation. It was a fine spring day. The clouds had cleared, and blue sky smiled down on us as I showed Philibert the niches where various types of plants grew.

"Plants live in communities," I explained, "just as people do. Even if I had to forage in an place I had never seen before, I would know where to look for communities of plants based simply on where they lived and what their neighboring plants were."

"That's quite remarkable," Philibert said.

"No, it's not remarkable." I demurred. "Most skilled herb women could do the same. Even housewives with their backyard gardens would have a good idea of which plants preferred to live next to each other."

"Of course." I saw that Philibert felt vaguely defensive. Perhaps he thought I was implying he lacked the basic knowledge of a peasant gardener. No matter. His thoughts were not my concern.

"Let us get started then." I trudged off to show him the plants of my open meadow.

Philibert's limp had gotten worse since the previous day. He struggled with his unwieldy basket. I watched as he strove to catch up with me. Without a word, I took the basket from him and looped it over my shoulder. It would speed things up. He did not object. By midday, when we paused for lunch, I was once again getting woozy from hunger. Philibert found a flat patch of ground, unrolled a small tablecloth, napkins, and a decanter of wine. I unpacked my single piece of hard, dark rye and a handful of currants.

"Is that all you have to eat?"

Shame tinted my cheeks pink, and I could not look at him or answer his question.

"Then you will share mine. After all, you carried my basket all morning. Consider it part of your payment." From under the linen cloth on his basket, he withdrew a slab of ham, half of a chicken, goat cheese, fluffy rolls filled with cream cheese, sliced radishes, and cucumbers. It was a princely feast, and I was stunned by the abundance of food.

My hunger overpowered my pride, and I helped myself sparingly to his victuals, not wanting to seem like the starving pauper that I was. At the end of the feast, he offered me a watered Beaujolais. Father did not drink, nor did he socialize at the village pub. We simply did not have the money to spare. I had never imbibed alcohol, and I recoiled at the idea. "No thank you," I said simply. I appreciated that he did not press me to drink the wine.

By the time the sun dropped behind the treetops, we were both bone tired but satisfied with a productive day. Philibert gave me his remaining bread and chicken and dropped three livre coins into my hand. It was more money than I had ever seen.

"Tomorrow?" he asked.

"Yes, tomorrow." I looked at the grass beneath my feet unwilling to let him see the relief in my eyes. "Thank you," I murmured softly, not wanting to seem ungrateful. In fact, I was very grateful. It had been a remarkable day. For the first time since Father died, curiosity made me wonder if there was another way for me to live, away from family, away from my little village. Meeting Philibert made me realize that there was a wide world out there. A little twinge of curiosity sparked in my heart, enticing me to see beyond the confines of this valley to the world beyond.

* * *

As the summer months unfolded, Philibert and I spent many hours together, dedicated to the shared purpose of gleaning herbal treasurers from the fields and forests. I had never met a man like Philibert. Though he had moments of insufferable arrogance, and a deeply ingrained sense of entitlement, he was a voracious student, with a brilliant mind. He vacillated from generosity and kindness to over-bearing haughtiness. I came to understand that on any given day he could display both of those traits in equal measure. Eventually, as he grew to value my expertise, his sense of superiority receded like a retreating army.

The summer sun warmed the earth, the air, and our feelings toward each other. Perhaps it was because of all the time we spent together, but our respect for each other matured. On one of those warm, sunny summer afternoons, as we rested on a verdant hillside to eat our midday meal, the conversation became personal again. Philibert had fallen into the habit of bringing extra bread and cheese, so I needn't be embarrassed by my obvious poverty.

"Have you ever been married?" he asked as he handed me a piece of bread torn from his loaf. The question surprised me, and my reaction was defensive. Why did he care? It was really none of his business.

"No, I have had no time for courting."

"Is that the only reason?"

"Yes. I have had very little opportunity, what with the crops, and herb hunting. I was a caretaker for my father, and now for my nieces and nephews. And besides, I did not need to be a seer to envision a future no different from my past, except I would no longer have control of my body, or my life. Now I am an old maid of twenty-four, and my suitors have found other wives."

I looked at him with a mixture of suspicion and reticence. Why were we entering this terra incognita of my personal life? "Now you must tell me about your marriage."

"It's rather complicated," he said. "I was on a plant collecting tour in the Alps when a rabid dog bit me. I became grievously ill. The Carthusian monks at the local monastery took me in and nursed me back to health. They are famous for their herbal medicines. I learned a great deal from them. At one point I concocted a cure-all with twenty-two ingredients, the monks still use. When I recovered sufficiently, I realized I should find a less taxing way to use my skills than clambering up and down mountains, so I decided to take on students interested in botany. A local landowner was looking for a tutor for his daughter, Antoinette, and she became my student. She is an intelligent woman of good breeding, and the daughter of a rich man. She had previously rejected several suitors and was getting too old to attract suitable marital prospects. Though her father had indulged his charming daughter, allowing her to reject several men, time was passing, and he needed to fulfill his fatherly responsibility by finding her a husband with good prospects. I was a Doctor of Medicine and a botanist with excellent connections and a promising future, and she would inherit wealth. It was a good match for both of us, and we were married."

"I see. I hope your marriage is a happy one." I genuinely wished this for him. He seemed to be fond of his wife, but I could not determine if he loved her. But then again, love was seldom a reason to marry. Philibert hinted that her domestic skills were lacking since she had grown up privileged, in a household with a large staff. Philibert was not wealthy enough to give her the kind of life she enjoyed as the daughter of a rich man, so Antoinette had a lot to learn about running a household. Philibert spoke of her with tenderness. It was clear he was fond of her, so I was not surprised when one day in late autumn Philibert announced that his wife was with child.

CHAPTER FOUR

CHANGES
1762

One April morning I stood on the familiar hillside redolent with the earthy smells of re-emerging life, scanning the slope for the familiar sight of Philibert with his basket slung over his back. Tortuous hours passed as anxious thoughts filled my head like thunderheads assembling to drop their torrent of rain.

Meeting him had become a reassuring habit, and I wondered if his interest had waned. Certainly, he was too much of a gentleman to leave me standing on the hillside without telling me he no longer needed my services. Yet, I worried that he might have been wearying of my company. I was just a simple herb woman, and he had no reason to meet me if he had his fill of this tiny corner of the world. At some point he would surely return to his well-placed friends in the parlors of Paris.

He often spoke with admiration of the luminaries and scholars at the Royal Garden. I tried to put Philibert out of my mind and go about my business. Spring was in its full glory. Asparagus was new and tender, butterflies danced among the wild rape flowers blanketing swaths of hillside in gold. Primrose pushed its shoots out from under a boulder eager to display its pale flowers as big as my palm. I scolded myself for thinking that I had become important to him. Imparting my knowledge of plants and their uses made me feel intelligent, even superior, and in his presence I could, for a few hours at least, escape my drab, mundane existence.

I tried to shrug off my disappointment with a sigh and turned my attention to my ever-reliable friends, the plants. I went about my business as I always had, harvesting the early spring edibles and recording the information in my notebook. But something in me had changed. I could no longer pretend Philibert meant nothing to me. His absence robbed the sunrise of its beauty. The crows who discussed my every move from their treetop perches mocked me with jeering calls. The pleasure I felt in my work now seemed like muddle-headed nonsense. I was a lonely, hopeless spinster peering from behind a veil of false hope. His absence ate at me like hunger and nagged me like a dog pawing me for attention.

Then one spring day, when blustery winds combed the clouds into wispy horse tails, he appeared. "Jeanne! There you are." He looked haggard; dark circles puddled under his eyes; he dragged his injured leg even more laboriously than usual. And he was thinner.

My eyebrows crept toward my hairline, wrinkling my brow. "What has happened? Are you alright? Did your wife have the baby?"

"Jeanne. I need your help. I don't know who else to ask."

"Ask for what? I have nothing. You know that."

"No, no, it's not like that. Antoinette is not doing well with this pregnancy. She needs more care than I can give her. She is weakening even as her time draws near. She can no longer manage the household or perform her daily tasks. Will you help us?"

I gasped involuntarily. That was the last thing I expected to hear.

"Dear Jeanne, I need someone to manage the household. Antoinette is weak and preoccupied with bringing this child into the world. She rarely leaves her bed. Will you come and stay at our home?"

My face flushed, and shock cramped my heart into a painful knot. "Don't you have a housekeeper who can do that?

"No, Antoinette never hired a housekeeper. She wanted to prove she was a competent woman and managed the house herself. I can hire a wetnurse if necessary, when the baby arrives, but I need a maid-of-all-works to cook, clean and care for Antoinette and the baby when it comes."

"But I know nothing of running a household such as yours!" I repeated, my voice growing shrill.

"I understand why you feel that way. My home is larger and perhaps more complicated than yours, but you are an intelligent, thoughtful woman. I'm sure you will learn quickly. I will tell you what needs to be done." His brow furrowed and his skin was pale. He appeared exhausted by worry. "Please Jeanne, I don't know who else to ask."

With his eyes misting up and threatening to spill over, he reached out, took my hand, and peered directly into my eyes. "In our short time together, I have come to rely on your storehouse of knowledge and meticulous attention to detail. I'm sure I can rely on you to maintain an orderly household for me as well."

I remained silent for many long moments, my mind a melting-pot of shock, fear, and reluctance. It was a tempting offer. I would never go hungry again, would not need to abide the endless grind of work, worry, and exhaustion I'd been enduring since my father's death. At day's end I would have a comfortable place to sleep. Philibert was, after all, a decent man. I respected him, and he respected me, despite our vastly different circumstances. I would no longer burden my sister's family. Kind as she was, her life would be easier without me.

"Yes," I said. "I will help you." The tension in his shoulders relaxed. Philibert was relieved, but my stomach churned with uncertainty. I was far less sure than I sounded. But I had made my choice. I would not turn back now.

THE VILLA

"Philibert, dear. Could you help me?" Antoinette called from her upholstered armchair. Philibert had just walked in the door from his day of botanizing. I longed to be with him, roaming the luxuriant countryside. I paid a high price for my security when I accepted this job. I had not anticipated how completely my life would change. I envied Philibert the freedom to roam and immerse himself in the miracles of the natural world. I should be outside in the sun, searching the hillsides and fields for herbs, medicinals, and edibles with Philibert. Instead, I rose before the sun, put a pot on the stove to boil, cooked, cleaned, and cared for Antoinette's needs.

I was confused about how to behave when Philibert and Antoinette carried on with their personal conversations in my presence. Should I leave them to their privacy? Should I stay, and pretend I did not hear them? They did not censor their conversations in front of me, in fact, they hardly acknowledged my presence at all. It was as if I had become invisible, no more worthy of notice than the tea service on the sideboard.

"Of course, darling. What do you need?" Philibert's eyes fell gently upon his petite wife. That is, she had been petite before she became pregnant. Now that her time was drawing near, her girth had expanded so much that she struggled to lace her shoes.

"Would you help me out of this chair?" She held her hand out to Philibert and smiled when he bowed with a flourish and took her hand. "I will be so happy when I deliver this child. He must be as big as a two-year-old, judging by how much I've grown. It's embarrassing. I can't even get out of my chair without help. I'm so uncomfortable. I can't sleep or take a deep breath easily. I lose my strength when I walk even a short distance."

"Poor dear, don't worry. Jeanne has dinner well in hand, and she is handling the business of managing the household very capably."

They both glanced at me as if they had just noticed me standing there at Antoinette's side. I tucked my chin against my breastbone, as if I'd been caught eavesdropping.

"Here, put your feet in my lap." Philibert lowered himself on to the ottoman to face her. He gently pushed up her skirts, exposing her ankles and calves. "Your legs are so swollen, no wonder you have trouble walking. A massage will make you feel better." Philibert began rubbing her calves from ankle to knee with sweeping upward strokes. Antoinette sighed with relief, and let her head loll back against the leather headrest as his strong hands kneaded her knotted muscles.

Philibert would not tell his wife as much, but as a doctor, he well knew that delivering a baby at the age of thirty-nine would most likely be difficult, especially since this was Antoinette's first pregnancy. She was a slight woman, barely taller than a twelve-year-old, and not physically robust. All he could do was find a good midwife, try to keep her comfortable and happy, and hope for the best.

April's full moon smiled benevolently into my open window, when a piercing scream coming from Philibert and Antoinette's bedroom sliced through the night's stillness yanking me from my sleep.

I tip-toed to their room and peeked around the corner of their open door. Antoinette's bed linen was soaked with a violent red ooze. I knew a certain amount of bleeding was expected in childbirth, but the sprawling stain I saw was surely not normal.

"Philibert, help!" Antoinette sounded more like a terrified animal than his well-bred wife. Another stabbing pain took her breath away and momentarily silenced her.

Antoinette reached for his hands and squeezed them with a startling strong grip. Her eyes skewered him, demanding his attention, and again, she pleaded for help. "It's alright, dear. I'll call the midwife." Philibert moved toward the door, saw me, and pointed a finger toward the servants' quarters where Yolanda, the midwife, slept. A month earlier, as the time of delivery approached, Philibert had taken the precaution of bringing a well-qualified midwife into the household. The villa was so far from town that it was much safer to have a woman skilled in childbirth on hand. I raced through the halls and unceremoniously shook her awake. Yolanda awoke instantly and we hurried to the master's bedroom.

"You may leave now, Monsieur Commerson. I can handle it from this point." Yolanda was as substantial as Antoinette was slight. She was buxom, with rosy cheeks, meaty arms and the unmistakable voice of authority. She elbowed Commerson out of her way as she hustled to Antoinette's bedside. Her face blanched when she realized Antoinette was hemorrhaging. When Antoinette saw the shock on Yolanda's face, she grasped the seriousness of her situation and shrieked wildly as fear overtook her.

"Go now," Yolanda commanded Philibert. "This is no place for a man."

"But I am a doctor."

Yolanda leveled a gaze as sharp as daggers at him. "How many babies have you delivered?"

Without a word Philibert withdrew, but he did not go far. Banished from the bedroom, Philibert clung to one side of the door frame, while I gripped the other, both of us attempting to be discreet as we watched the drama unfold. Yolanda's urgency alarmed me. Surely, she had seen many births and by now was inured to the lurid birthing process.

Seeing us clinging to the door frame, she commanded. "If you are going to lurk at the doorway, make yourself useful and bring us hot water,"

Despite the fact that a pitcher of water and an ewer were in plain sight on the bedstand, running to warm water would give us something to do. I grabbed the pitcher, ran to the kitchen and filled it with hot water from the stove, and with Philibert at my heels hustled back to the bedroom.

"Just close your eyes dear and breathe deeply." Yolanda's crooned, her voice was like honey, smooth and reassuring. She did her best to calm the panic-stricken Antoinette as she laid a warm, damp cloth on the laboring mother's forehead and pressed a towel into her hands. "When the next pain begins, take this towel and squeeze it as hard as you can."

Yolanda knew squeezing a towel would have little practical effect, but it gave Antoinette an outlet for her fear and pain. When the next paroxysm rocked her, she twisted the damp towel in her shaking hands as if she intended to strangle life out of it. Yolanda swabbed Antoinette's forehead with water again. The labor went on for hours until Antoinette was too exhausted to squeeze the towel any longer, and she let it drop to the ground.

Yolanda's experienced hands roamed over Antoinette's belly gauging the baby's position. "This baby wants to come out the wrong way. Now, do as I say," she said putting her face near Antoinette's to assure herself Antoinette heard her.

"Luckily the baby's head is down, so it is not going to come out feet first. That is good news, but it is facing upward toward your belly instead of down toward your spine. I have seen this position before, and I can deal with it. Your job is to push when I tell you to."

Antoinette made only a garbled response. Yolanda inserted her fingers into Antoinette's womb, snagged the baby's ears and turned his face upward. Antoinette screamed like the hounds of hell. When the next contraction seized Antoinette, Yolanda hollered. "Now Antoinette, now! PUSH!"

Antoinette howled as she strained to do as she was told. Despite her heroic effort, the baby's progress stalled halfway through the birth canal. The baby could not retreat, and it refused to descend further.

"Bear down!" Yolanda was sweating now as she applied downward pressure to Antoinette's belly. Despite Yolanda's efforts, the baby made no more progress. Antoinette's howls weakened to moans and then ebbed into muffled groans. Antoinette was fading and

Yolanda needed to intervene. This situation was dangerous for both mother and baby.

She carefully inserted her fingers inside Antoinette's body again. She curled them behind the baby's ears and when the next contraction came, she shouted. "Push! Now! As hard as you can!" Yolanda pulled as hard as Antoinette pushed. "Keep going, keep going! Don't stop now. We are almost there." After three more contractions, the baby's slick body finally slid into the light of day. Antoinette fell into a dead faint.

"Monsieur Commerson," Yolanda's voice was hoarse and raspy. "I know you are cowering beyond that door. Come and meet your baby boy." As if to demonstrate its vigor, the baby let out an ear-splitting cry.

"What's wrong with him? His head is like a cone and his face is as red as a ripe apple."

"He has just endured an arduous birth. He will be fine. But your wife has lost a lot of blood and will need time to recover. Do you have anyone to look after her?"

"Yes," he replied. His eyes slid from the baby to me. "Jeanne has been helping us for the last few months. She is capable, and level-headed. I don't know what we would do without her."

My heart hammered relentlessly against my ribs like a blacksmith at his forge. Philibert's faith in me seemed unwarranted, and in my heart, I wanted nothing to do with this messy business. Keeping the house clean and the family fed was one thing, but this barbaric process of giving birth to a baby inspired only nausea in me rather than awe or joy.

Philibert's expression reflected his helpless fear, and desperation. With the crisis over, a wave of relief crashed over me, and I knew I could not deny him my best efforts. "I will be here to help you and Antoinette," I choked on the words.

"Good," the ever-practical Yolanda said coolly. "Your wife will not be able to return to her normal household activities for quite some time."

Antoinette struggled to regain a tenuous hold on consciousness. "My baby," she simpered weakly.

Yolanda brought the baby to Antoinette's breast. Though the newborn searched for the nipple, Antoinette was too weak to help him suckle his first meal. Yolanda guided the infant's mouth to the nipple and held him there until he latched on and began nursing intently.

The following days passed in a fog. Antoinette remained feeble. She did her best to feed the baby, but she weakened so rapidly that soon she could no longer even cradle him securely in her arms. Her skin was ghostly pallid and hung loosely around her face like drapery. It was the first time she looked every day of her thirty-nine years. Even her smallest movements were an effort, and she never left her bed.

Philibert stayed resolutely at her side, sleeping in a chair next to her bed, taking his meals at the nearby writing desk, and caressing her face with moist cloths as she lay inert and unresponsive. She never regained full consciousness, and within the week, she was dead.

The death hollowed Philibert out, and he wandered the halls like a specter, with expressionless, glazed eyes, and a stiff, wooden bearing. He was so incapacitated he could not bring himself to make funeral arrangements.

The responsibility for Antoinette's funeral fell to Yolanda and me. Yolanda was not happy about it and complained that this was not part of her work.

"It's not part of my work either," I grumbled. "That man is like a helpless child. If called upon to do something he does not want to do, he simply leaves the room and goes somewhere else. This is not what I was hired to do."

Yolanda patted my hand, "Someone must take responsibility for the man and the child, and you are the only one here."

"It has been several days already, and he has done nothing to arrange for her burial. She can't just lay there in her deathbed." Yolanda complained.

"I know. We must deal with this as soon as possible. I buried my father," I said. The words stabbed my heart like a dagger. "I will call the priest and make arrangements."

Antoinette's funeral was nothing at all like my father's and I needed Philibert's help. That day, I confronted him. "Antoinette's family needs to know she has died. They will want a proper ceremony for her. If you can't do it yourself, you must contact them and ask for their help. You must give her the ceremony she deserves."

Philibert took a deep breath and sat down at his desk to write to Antoinette's father and brother, then sent for a messenger to deliver the sad news. Together Yolanda and I washed Antoinette's emaciated body and wound it in a fine linen shroud. Her father arranged for a bier to carry her casket back to the family's mausoleum where a niche awaited her.

It was a somber procession. Philibert, in a black woolen suit, sat like a statue upon his horse, while I, in a simple black cotton dress, walked behind him carrying the motherless infant. My mind wandered to her family in Charollais, many hours away. Were they mourning? Did they even attempt to come to her funeral? It was so unfortunate. She deserved better, I thought. After the funeral Philibert wandered the halls around the villa like a specter, with expressionless, glazed eyes, and slumped shoulders.

As promised, Yolanda found a wet nurse for the little boy Philibert named Archambaud. The child fussed, and cried continually, craving the love, attention, from a nurturing mother he needed. Philibert kept his distance from the baby. Yolanda saw the tragic direction Philibert was taking with the child. Never one to mince words, she finally confronted him.

"This baby needs mothering," she told Philibert. "If you cannot give the child the love he needs, you need to find someone who can. I cannot stay with you any longer. I have other mothers who need me, and I have already spent too much time here."

"I hired a wet nurse." Philibert whined defensively. "Can't she care for the child?"

"Yes, for a while she can, but her own child needs nurturing as well. Soon it will be up to you to make more permanent arrangements for him."

Philibert stumbled through the next weeks as if sleepwalking. His head throbbed. He finally realized an infant requires round-the-clock care. He never imagined he would be responsible for a newborn. That was a woman's place, not his. He longed to get back to his normal routine and felt the pull of the green hillsides and the open meadow as a river feels the pull of gravity.

Yolanda, however, had washed her hands of him. The wet nurse went through the motions of caring for the baby but spent less and less time with him as the weeks went by. Philibert had no one else to call upon, so he turned to me. He had become steadily more dependent on me since our chance meeting two years ago. It hurt me to see how helpless he was now. Though I had no desire to nurture an infant, neither could I see him waste away, so I asked the wet nurse what I needed to do.

"It is not so difficult," she explained. "Buy a goat with babies of her own. Simply milk her as you would a cow. Dip a soft rag into the milk and give it to the baby to suck upon. It may take a little practice, but soon enough, it will become as easy as watching water run downhill."

I had helped my sister care for her several children, and I knew what raising children entailed. There would be dirty diapers, baby vomit, midnight rocking, and sleep deprived days of utter exhaustion. I thought I could take care of Archambaud's basic needs, but not the way a mother would. I did the best I could, going through the motions, but I did not develop a bond or affection for the baby. Nonetheless, Archambaud grew into a healthy but lonely toddler, lacking nothing except his father's time, attention, and love.

CHAPTER FIVE

THE CHILD
1764

In the two years since Antoinette's death, I petitioned Philibert to get household help many times.

"Wouldn't I be more helpful as your field assistant than as a cook, maid, or nanny? I miss our time together scouring the fields for plants."

He reluctantly consented to allowing me to get help with tasks I could accomplish indoors. I imposed as many of my motherly duties on the cook and the maid as I could, to free up a little time to do what I loved. During those stolen minutes Philibert taught me the Latin nomenclature and protocol for labeling botanical samples. Though I had learned my letters and basic math from Father Luc, my education was rudimentary. As a child I went to school when I could be spared from field work. I would have loved to stay in school forever, but my responsibilities to my family's welfare made it difficult. In winter I trudged through the snow whenever I could, and tramped the treacherous, muddy roads in spring to attend the classroom set up by the Father Luc. I attended school often enough to learn the basics.

My father was unlettered. He understood all too well that not being able to read doomed him to a lifetime of manual labor, as it did to all the other poor peasants of La Comelle. Despite this, or perhaps because of it, he saw the value of education, even for girls. Learning basic arithmetic could help a housewife bargain in the market and not be fleeced by dishonest vendors. Being able to read allowed his children to study the Bible.

For my part, a basic education made me a more valuable assistant to Philibert. After his botanizing forays, Philibert and I would stand side-by-side, our heads bent over a long table covered with dozens of pressed plants, all neatly labeled with their Latin names, and the dates and places they were collected. Scattered on the floor around us were the wooden frames of field presses used to dry, flatten, and preserve our specimens. We used most of the villa's rooms for our plant specimens. It worked well for us but was totally inappropriate for a Archambaud, now a toddler.

Now two-years old, he rampaged through the morning room, the great room, and the study where we were working as if fleeing a dragon, waving a ladle, and shrieking like an injured puppy, while the cook, a rotund matron of a certain age, waddled behind him in pursuit.

"Archie, give that back to me right now, or I will use it to paddle your backside when I catch you," the cook squawked.

Philibert and I sighed in unison. I put down the magnifying glass with which I had been studying the subtle differences between a Monkey orchid and a Lady orchid.

"What are we going to do with him?" I complained. "I know he is just a little boy, but he is a hurricane on legs, a raging tempest."

"He is just trying to get attention," Philibert responded. "The cook does not have the time to attend to him, and Archie is not her concern."

"Yes, and that's the problem. He is supposed to be my concern. You expect me to be the nanny, the household manager, and your botany partner. He needs more attention than either of us can give him, and I simply can't be a good mother to him. He is a great distraction."

"Ah well," Philibert shrugged off my complaints. Since Antoinette's death I had become the woman of the house, overseeing its maintenance, and expenses.

"I am also expected to manage the boy." Philibert showed no sympathy for my plight. He saw all those tasks as 'women's work.' Women's work consisted of the many tasks women were simply expected to do, what women had always done, and nothing to complain about. In his view, the man of the house provided monetary support and little else. Since inheriting Antoinette's wealth, supporting the family financially had ceased to be a concern for him, and therefore he was free to pursue the life of a gentleman scientist, a life he had always dreamed of. He had no intention of helping with Archambaud.

"Perhaps tomorrow you can take him to the market with you. That should divert him for a while," Philibert offered.

I furrowed my brow and made a sour expression. "That's another matter entirely. Do you have any idea what I go through when I am out in public?"

Philibert gave me a sidelong glance and shrugged. "I suppose I will hear about it whether I want to or not."

"Since Antoinette's death, the townswomen consider me a disreputable hanger on, a gold digger, just two steps away from being a "kept" woman. Think about it as they do, Philibert. In their eyes, I am a single woman living under the roof of a single man, taking care of a household and a child, neither of which are mine. Since I don't leave at night to return to my own home, it's as clear as a cloudless morning that I am living in sin and taking advantage of a grieving widower. When I greet them, they raise their chins and turn their heads away as if they smell something malodorous. I see them huddled in little groups whispering to each other, clicking their tongues just loudly enough for me to hear. When I get close enough to understand their words, their voices drop, and all conversation ceases. At the market the vendors refuse to negotiate with me as they would with the other women so I must pay higher prices."

Philibert placed his hands on my shoulders and turned me toward him laying his index finger over my lips to silence me. "Do not worry, my dear. Their opinions do not matter to me at all. Every day my respect and fondness for you grows. You know I want you here with me. I agree that the boy disrupts our work. There must be some solution, so just let me think this through and I'll find a way."

I rested my head against his chest listening to the comforting thumping of his heartbeat. I wanted to believe him. Since Antoinette's death, our relationship had matured into a glorious flower in full bloom, I had never known the love of a man. Our love, born of a shared purpose, mutual respect, and daily proximity, created a sweet harmony of affection and desire. I had not expected this to happen. Previously, when I heard women pine for lost lovers, or wax rhapsodic over the joys of physical love, I could not fathom what all the fuss was about. I thought it was feather-headed foolishness. But gradually my feelings for Philibert had matured into love, physical love. His lovemaking was slow and tender, as effortless as snow melting in spring, the most natural thing in the world. He was still sometimes thoughtless and arrogant, but I could tell that, in his way, he loved me.

In the years before I met Philibert I had worked long and hard to earn my keep, and be a help to my sister, fighting my own private war to beat back hunger, exhaustion, and constant uncertainty. With Philibert, I found a partner who could take that responsibility off my shoulders. For the first time in my life, I could lift my head and look forward with clear eyes to a hopeful future. I had enough time and energy to nurture our relationship and be a partner in his botanical work. I felt strong and confident - that is until I had to march out among the petty gossips who delighted in slandering me.

When I first moved into Philibert and Antoinette's household my only intention was to assist them in whatever way was needed. I had no expectations, no plans, no thoughts of the future. I wanted only to be as useful as I could be. As Antoinette became frailer, I assumed more responsibility, and when the poor woman died, a mere three days after her son's birth, I was ill-prepared to take over. I suddenly went from being the maid to raising a newborn and managing the entire household. I lacked experience, and for several months, I floundered.

Philibert saw my struggle. One day, after I had fed the baby and tucked him into his cradle Philibert sought me out in the nursery. He looked down at the child and took my hand. "Dear Jeanne," he said. "I think I have an idea that will help you cope with all the responsibilities you bear."

"Really?" I smiled. "Do you know some alchemy that can make me into three people?"

He smiled. "I don't know alchemy, but I know a woman. She is old, but I think she can help. Her name is Camile. She served Antoinette's family since Antoinette was a toddler. Perhaps I can persuade her to help care for the child."

"Oh Philibert. That would be a great relief."

Camile was old indeed, her face a map of wrinkles, a nearly bald head enveloped in a tattered headscarf, and shoulders as rounded as an overturned bowl. But she was spritely and good-natured. She patiently tried to teach me how to be a surrogate mother to a two-year-old boy.

As soon as Camile picked him up, little Archie quieted immediately. When she handed him to me, he squirmed, pushed his little arms against my shoulders and tried to escape. It was clear to her that I lacked the maternal feelings that were supposed to be natural to women. In her estimation, my chilliness toward the boy was both a moral failing and a character defect.

Her sojourn at our home was short-lived. She did what she could but, just as the midwife could not stay with us indefinitely, Camile also wanted to return to her family. She was old and aspired only to a rocking chair next to a warm fire. It was again up to me to care for little Archie.

* * *

I wanted desperately to please Philibert and show him I could be as competent at managing our household as I was at ferreting out herbs. As the months passed, I strove to adapt and he respected my efforts.

In some ways our lives remained the same. Each morning, we left Archambaud with the cook as we set out to search the hillsides, meadows, and woodlots for plants to label and analyze. Working with Philibert rekindled in me that special warmth I remembered from herb hunting with my sister and Auntie Juliette. Philibert made me feel appreciated and valued – special. Though I tried to ignore the rising tide of fondness I felt for him, I could no longer deny that I was falling in love with Philibert.

One warm spring evening, after I had tucked Archambaud into bed, and the house grew quiet, I sidled up to Philibert and placed a tender kiss on his cheek.

"Well, well," he said. "What's this all this about?"

"You have given me so much," I purred. "I have only one possession worthy enough to express my affection for you." I dipped my hand into my pocket and took out my small, black notebook. Row upon row of tiny script filled its pages. Philibert examined it closely, his expression changed from curiosity to wonderment as the import of what he was holding dawned on him. The handwritten entries were the record of every plant I had collected, the sum of my exhaustive knowledge over my many years of exploring my surroundings. Each entry had the date each specimen was collected, its location, and medicinal use. It was as precious to me as a king's jewels

"Surely nothing like this exists in any library in the world," I said, and I pushed it toward him on my outstretched hand.

"My god!" Philibert exclaimed. "Is this what I think it is?" He had watched me making meticulous notes every time we went out hunting plants. It was a deeply intrenched habit, worthy of the most conscientious botany student. I knew this unassuming little notebook would be a godsend for his work. I hoped he knew it too.

"It is the only thing of value I own. I want you to have it as a symbol of my love and devotion to you. You have changed my life."

Philibert dragged his eyes away from the notebook, carefully placing it on the table, and gathered me into his arms. "You can't possibly know how much this means to me. You will be my treasured partner and lover to the end of my days." It was as close to a marriage proposal as he ever got, and I was satisfied with it.

The next morning, Philibert reached across the breakfast table and took my hand.

"I have worked it out," he said. "You need not put up with the slights of the local women any longer. I have thought it through. There is nothing keeping us here. Why don't we leave this place? There are far better opportunities for me in Paris. I can prepare to leave as soon as possible." He beamed at me, so sure I would be overjoyed. And I was overjoyed, but it wasn't going to be simple.

"There is one problem." I ran my hand over my dress, pressing the fabric tight enough to reveal the shapely curve of my belly. The bump was still small enough to hide beneath my skirts, but it was unmistakable.

Philibert's shoulders fell, and a surly scowl replaced his optimistic smile. "This is most unfortunate." He scolded me like a school master, disappointed at his prize student's failings, like it was all my fault.

My face reddened as if I had been slapped. He did not offer me one kind word, not one gesture of sympathy, certainly no joyful acknowledgement of becoming a father again. "This will never do. You are unmarried and there are strict rules regarding illegitimate pregnancies. Because you are unmarried, you must file a certificate of pregnancy." He was all business now, like a surgeon repairing a wound. He lost himself in thought for a few minutes then picked up the conversation. "This is what you need to do. I will arrange a trip for you to go the registration office, as required, to complete the necessary paperwork. They will ask you for the name of the father. I forbid you to name me."

I had not foreseen this response. I was shocked by his officious practicality, devoid of any warmth or sympathy, confused by his vindictive attitude, scolding me like an errant child, as if this pregnancy was all my fault and he had nothing to do with it. It was all I could do to suppress my tears. Unlike Philibert who suffered no conflicting emotions, I was torn apart. I could not risk an unwanted pregnancy upsetting our already complicated relationship, yet I felt the pull of the unborn baby in my heart. Even though he did not pay much attention to Archie, I somehow thought our baby would bring us closer. How could I have been so deluded?

My position was already precarious. Although I could not bury the stirrings of love for this baby, my baby, I could not allow my heart to overpower my head. I loved Philibert and needed him. I knew he would make his decision with little regard for my feelings, and I was powerless. Without him, I was no one. I had no way of supporting myself, much less a baby. Would I have to return to my sister's home in shame? She would be furious and might well turn me out.

His hard-heartedness startled me, and a choking panic rose in my throat. Many men, I knew, abandoned their lovers when pregnancy complicated their cozy relationship. If Philibert did that, where would I be?

"I know this is unexpected, and I am sorry this happened. I don't want this disruption any more than you do. No one needs to know about this." I apologized, sounding piteous, even to myself. A bubble of resentment rose in me. I was not the only one to be blamed for an unintended pregnancy. Why wasn't he apologizing to me as well? I expected at least some sympathy. But he blithely disposed of the problem without a single twinge of remorse.

In the following days we exchanged very few words about the situation. He took the matter in hand and dealt with it quickly and efficiently. He was right about getting the necessary certificate of pregnancy. It was required that every woman who became pregnant complete a declaration of pregnancy. For me, it meant I must take a long carriage ride to the nearest registration office, twenty miles away. It would be inconvenient to say the least. A woman traveling alone would be exposed to all kinds of potential dangers, from predatory men, and insulting, suspicious fellow travelers, to being overcharged by the coachman. In my entire life, I had never been more than a few miles from home.

"I have found two well-respected men of my acquaintance to chaperone you on your trip to the registration office. One is a prominent landowner in this vicinity, and the other is a doctor."

I inhaled noisily. "But I don't know these men. How do I know they are trustworthy?"

"They are professional men, and they are doing me a great favor agreeing to accompany you."

Our eyes locked. His were piercing and as cold as ice. Mine were fearful and angry. We were at an impasse, and I realized how powerless I was. I should have been grateful, and I was. But Philibert was arrogant and unsympathetic, without a hint of compassion.

Now I found myself in a crowded carriage flanked by two professionals whose haughty bearing highlighted the disparity in our social status. I had never met these men, but Philibert knew them well enough to impose upon them to accompany me. It was a nasty business indeed.

Not long after filing the certificate of pregnancy, Philibert made another decision that would change my life forever. After weeks of exchanging letters with his most prestigious friends - Carl Linnaeus, Francois Voltaire, and Le Comte de Buffon, he burst into the parlor waiving a letter over his head. "We are moving to Paris!" He was elated. "And soon! There is an opportunity for me at the Jardin de Roi that I simply cannot pass up. I can't cloister myself in this backwater forever."

I jerked up from the couch like a marionette whose strings had been pulled. "We're moving to Paris?"

"If I am to advance my career as a botanist, I can't waste away in a place like La Comelle. I must associate with well-respected men in my profession. This position will give me that opportunity."

"I understand, I do. It's just that . . ." My voice trailed off and I looked down as I ran my hands over my expanding belly.

"First we must deal with your pregnancy and Antoinette's son." Philibert charged on like a bull attacking the toreador's red cape. "I will take Archambaud to Antoinette's brother, Father Francois Beau. You've met him. He is the parish priest who officiated at her funeral."

I did remember Father Beau, a good man, soft-spoken, with large dark eyes and a mild demeanor, who exuded empathy and concern for his parishioners.

"He is a decent fellow, reliable and good-hearted. He will tend to the boy's best interests, for his sister's sake." His eyes ran over my body. "We will deal with your pregnancy when we get to Paris." For a moment, his eyes softened, and he reached for my hand. "Everything will be alright. You must understand how important this is to my career."

That night Philibert embraced me as ardently as he ever had. He took me in his arms and made tender love to me. I was confused by this man who was arrogant, aloof, one moment and sweet and loving the next. Afterward, I lay by his side trying to absorb the contradictions of my situation. I didn't understand how moving to Paris would make my situation any better. But Philibert's confidence in the future along with the warmth of his body calmed me. I only knew that I teetered on the precipice of an entirely new life.

CHAPTER SIX

PARIS
1764

At first, riding the two hundred miles to Paris by stagecoach had sounded like an exciting adventure, nothing like the sober trip to register my illegitimate pregnancy. Then, I felt like a prisoner flanked by two stalwart wardens escorting me to my punishment. Now I was full of hope. The journey to Paris took four full days. Philibert and I were crushed between other travelers, their luggage, several sacks of grain, and bulging mail bags. The seating compartment, suspended over the wheels cradled by two heavy thongs, bounced mercilessly over the rough roads. The smell of sweating people and horses, and dust from the road permeated the air making my eyes sting and my stomach roil. I avoided taking a deep breath for fear I would vomit. I thanked heaven for the mild temperatures and balmy breezes. At least we did not face sweltering summer heat or the icy grip of winter.

My unborn baby, now big enough to cause discomfort under normal circumstances, danced inside my belly, agitated by the jostling carriage. Tiny feet kicked at my stomach, elbows dug into my ribs, and an increasingly large head squeezed my lungs. I was green with nausea and barely able to move in the confined space. Our only respites were the wayside stations where the weary horses were unharnessed and traded for fresh ones. During these short intervals we had a brief opportunity to step out onto solid ground, stretch, and occasionally buy a chunk of crusty rye bread, apples, cheese, or wine from the roadside vendors. But I dared not eat too much for fear of upsetting the delicate balance between persistent nausea and active vomiting.

Philibert was blithely unaffected by my discomfort. He chattered about the rural scenery, and the wonderful sights we would encounter in Paris.

"You simply can't conceive of the size of Paris," he enthused. "The grandeur of the palaces will astound you. All the important men of our time live in Paris. The Royal Academy of Science attracts the top luminaries–scientists, mathematicians, philosophers, astronomers, and botanists like me, interested in natural philosophy. The culture is rich and varied, with theater performances, symphony orchestras, and opera." His eyes were misty with anticipation. "We will enjoy evenings in the salons of the most esteemed luminaries, scientists, artists, and philosophers, who gather for intellectual camaraderie. Have you ever been to the theater?" He knew, of course I hadn't, but he rambled on. "You will love it. We will want to settle as close to the Jardin do Roi as we can. Their collection of plants is unparalleled."

Philibert's enthusiasm left me cold. I knew nothing about theaters, concerts, or art. My dearth of sophistication, my peasant patois, my lack of social graces, and the indelicacy of my every gesture marked me as a lower-class hay seed. It made me wish I could hide in a closet. The last thing I wanted was to embarrass myself or Philibert.

"No one knows me there and people will immediately take me for a country bumpkin," I worried.

"Don't worry, I will buy you new clothes and perhaps bring in an aesthetician to school you in hair and makeup styles." Philibert offered.

His enthusiasm was getting the best of him, he would never give that much thought to how fashionable I appeared. That was probably for the best. My goal was to quietly fade into the background. I was not interested in Paris fashions or beauty standards. My brown hair was thin and straight, easily braided and coiled around my head. Perhaps I might exchange my weary, wilting peasant's bonnet for a new, white linen cap with a frilled edge. That, at least, might prevent people from looking at me as if I were a washer woman. But that's as far as I cared to go with any personal beautification project. I didn't see the point of fussing over a woman as plain as myself.

There was a positive aspect to the different cultural milieu. "In Paris, perhaps the people will not look down their noses at me because I am with child."

"Oh, my dear, certainly not. These people are worldly and sophisticated. Why, several of the most well-known and respected men live openly with their lovers. You will see. We will continue our work together free from the narrow-minded attitudes of peasants. Who are they to judge us?"

I appreciated his reassurances, well-intentioned as they were, but I was not moved. I struggled to keep my mind open to the possibility that I might like Paris.

We arrived on a blustery day when the colorful leaves of the late summer trees floated down like falling butterflies. Within a few days, Philibert had located a second-floor apartment for us in the Rue des Boulangers near the Jardin de Roi, on a street that seemed to me as royal as the garden itself. Our building housed eight spacious apartments, four on the first floor, and four on the second. They were arranged around a well-tended courtyard where the proprietress lovingly nurtured her garden of vegetables and flowers. For me, the garden was a welcome sight and eased the anxiety caused by moving from a peaceful pastoral setting to a noisy, smelly, bustling metropolis. I followed Philibert up the stairs to a solid oak door embellished with a filigreed door handle. He opened the lock and threw the door wide, gesturing for me to step inside. I crossed the threshold gingerly, took three steps and stopped abruptly. My head swiveled around like a Barn owl searching for mice. The coved ceiling was tastefully ornamented and painted gold, as were the moldings, and the fireplace mantle. The spacious two-bedroom dwelling exuded calm and grandeur.

"Are you sure this is the right place?" I said as I gawked in wonder.

"Of course, my dear. Money is no longer an issue we need to worry about. I know it must seem like a palace to you, but our Parisian visitors will consider it quite modest. Do you like it?"

Speech evaded me as I crept inside. Two enormous windows lurking behind heavy drapes drew me toward them like a moth to the flame. I tugged back the weighty velvet. Tall casement sashes made of wavy glass resting in mullioned panes stood like stewards inviting me to enjoy the view. I stepped out onto a small, curved balcony jutting out over the teeming street, braced myself against the limestone railing, and breathed in the pungent smells of Paris. The cacophony of sounds and scents created by a half million souls living cheek by jowl along the crowded streets assaulted my senses. The neighborhood pulsed with life – horses high-stepped through the streets pulling carriages, farmers pushed carts loaded with newly harvested vegetables, palanquins with heavily draped windows supported by four muscular men surged through the street below. Laundry draped over balconies dried in the honeyed glow of autumn sunshine. Children chased a ball through the crowded streets below, while dogs nipped at their heels. Street vendors loudly hawked their wares, singing out the praises of their products. All of it created an air of frenzied activity and excitement.

I turned toward Philibert, who stood as still as statuary. He stared intently at me, reading my reaction. I must have radiated awe and perhaps delight, as he opened his arms and gathered me in into his embrace.

"This is our home now, the place where we will start our new life together, as partners and lovers," he breathed into my ear. I sank into his arms, nuzzling his neck, relieved and renewed, ready for whatever came next.

The first weeks passed, and I did my best to accustom myself to my new life. I ambled through the neighborhoods ferreting out markets and shops. Philibert had been right, despite my now prominent belly, no one gave me a second glance as I walked the narrow streets. I was invisible to them, a ghost among many ghosts haunting the streets. My anonymity was a mixed blessing. It was true that no-one judged or castigated me for my shameful condition. No one realized I was unwed, and no one cared. On the other hand, everyone had lives of their own, so no one offered me a warm greeting or a hand of friendship. I had no sisters or nieces or nephews who knew me through and through. Despite the throngs bustling around me, I felt lonely.

Some days later, Philibert walked to the nearby Jardin de Roi and called upon le Comte de Buffon, the director. He came home vibrating with hopeful energy.

"Buffon and I met! We had an excellent discussion. He remembered me because Carl Linnaeus generously provided a recommendation for me. Remember I told you about him and his revolutionary system for classifying species? Buffon is working on a voluminous oeuvre, called *Natural History*, a mighty compendium covering the entire natural world. He has already published fifteen volumes; can you believe it? He graciously told me he was happy I was here and he would benefit from my knowledge." Philibert beamed.

"That sounds very promising. How does he intend to use *your* store of knowledge?" He was too excited to notice my emphasis on the word *your.* Philibert knew very well that his store of knowledge was *our* store of knowledge, but I didn't expect to be recognized for my contributions. He was the scholar, after all, and I was the peasant herb woman.

Our association with the Jardin du Roi turned out to be very productive and satisfying. Just as Philibert predicted, our move to Paris opened new doors for us. The Jardin regularly sent plant specimens to our home so we could conduct research on them. Soon our apartment became a botanical laboratory filled with plants of all kinds - exotics from far-flung lands, potted local cultivars, dried plants hanging from strings, tuberous plants, low crawling plants, and small upright trees tucked into corners. We were working side by side once again, immersed in research on a par with other great botanists.

My favorite challenge was studying plants that closely resembled each other but were not of the same species. I happily immersed myself in analysis of the details that defined them, their veins, stems, roots, buds, and blossoms. Our work at the Jardin de Roi involved evaluating the similarities and differences between the exotics and our well-known native species. The thrill of adding to the knowledge of the natural world returned, and I regained my sense of purpose.

I excelled at analyzing resemblances and differences between plants from disparate locations. Did plants from the Atlas Mountains of Africa resemble plants from the Altai mountains of Russia or our own Alps? Did plants with edible tubers that grew in England need the same soil types as those grown in Albania? As a team, Philibert and I were a perfect match. My skill for meticulous record-keeping and my keen powers of observation complimented Philibert's knowledge of the Linnaean principles of taxonomy and his comprehensive knowledge of the Mediterranean. We were a formidable pair.

Our unfettered immersion in the wonders of botanical research ended abruptly on the day my water broke, and painful contractions began. With Antoinette's experience fresh in his memory, Philibert had the foresight to prepare for this inevitable inconvenience. He solicited the opinion of Henri Rousseau, whose long-time, live-in lover had delivered five of his illegitimate children. Who better to ask for help finding a capable and superbly discreet midwife than the scandalous Rousseau? I was grateful for Philibert's solicitude, and I was confident I would be in the hands of a capable, well-respected midwife. Nonetheless, I had no illusions about the dangers and risks of childbirth.

I had given a lot of thought to maintaining our respectable image and steeled myself for the ordeal. As I grew larger, I spent less time outdoors, and when I did venture out, I padded myself with extra clothing giving the impression I was putting on weight all over, not just in my belly. I was determined not to wail, scream, and carry on as so many other women did. Calling attention to this birth among my neighbors could only draw unwanted attention, and harm Philibert's reputation. If I had relied on him in La Comelle, my dependency on him here in Paris was complete.

The midwife quickly and efficiently provisioned the second bedroom with everything needed for a new mother and baby. When labor began in earnest, the pain became all-consuming as my body turned itself inside out. The midwife had prepared cool, wet cloths for my forehead, sips of water, and a drop or two of laudanum when the pain was at its worst. Luckily, it was an uncomplicated delivery. My body had its own inexorable task to complete, and it served me well. The baby and I came through the ordeal admirably, and by the time his little head emerged, I was sweaty and exhausted but transported by pride and relief. The baby squalled, impatient to enter the world of the living. When I put him to my breast, he voraciously attached and lapped up the nourishment like a barn cat at a milk pail.

The day following the birth, as I lay ensconced among the pillows, Philibert crept quietly into my room. My hair billowed around my shoulders, and though my face was pale, it glowed with health. My heart expanded when I saw his expression transform into wonder and awe as he saw me cradling the tiny baby boy. This was his son, and for a few moments his heart opened. He gently sat on the edge of the bed and smoothed my hair.

"He is a fine baby, and you will love him, as all mothers do," he crooned. "Nature has imbued women with a fierce instinct to love and protect their infants. Believe me, I understand. But you must not become too attached. You know what needs to happen next." My heart sank. Of course I remembered, but now that the little one was in my arms, I wanted only to keep him and love him. I was wrong about my lack of maternal instincts. It seemed that my icy indifference only applied to Archambaud.

"I'm sure you remember what it was like living with Archambaud in La Comelle." My chin dropped to my chest. I recalled the chaos that swirled around the child. Yes, I remembered. I was happy when Philibert found another home for that rambunctious boy. But this was different. This was *my* son.

All the soft-heartedness dropped from his demeanor, and he became the embodiment of unemotional practicality as he had when he consigned Archambaud to Antoinette's brother, the priest. "He will have your surname, not mine. For the time being he will need nourishment from you to get a good start in life. But you must choose between him and me. If you choose to keep him, you can move back to your sister. If you want to continue our life together, the good nuns at the foundling hospital will provide for him."

I could not look him in the eye. I gazed into the angelic face of my perfect baby sleeping in my arms. As soundless as when I gave birth, I now silently poured out my tears.

"There is no need to feel guilty," Philibert said, mistaking my tears for guilt. "Thousands of mothers have had thousands of reasons to take this path. But the decision is yours."

"Yes, of course, you are right." I drew a deep, shuddering breath, squeezed my eyes to staunch the tears, and whispered barely audibly "I choose you."

Philibert caressed my hair again, stood, and left the room, quietly closing the door behind him. When he was gone, I hugged my baby to my breast, rocked back and forth, and heaved great, silent sobs. I cried for a very long time, until I had wrung every tear from my eyes, leaving only dry-eyed despair. One month later, I delivered a tightly swaddled bundle into the arms of the good nuns at the foundling hospital.

"His name is Jean-Pierre Baret," I told the sister who opened the door. I could not choke out another word, nor meet her soft brown eyes. Her gaze held all the compassion in the world, but it could not soothe my troubled spirit.

"Don't worry, we will do our best to find a good foster home for him. If your circumstances change, you can return, and we will know where you can find him." The doe-eyed sister reached out to gather the infant into her arms. "Be at peace. God sees you and loves both you and your baby. All will be well. We will find a loving foster family for him. He will grow up with everything he needs."

I stood tall, masking my emotions with a look of determination. I told myself I was doing the right thing, the only thing that made sense. What kind of life could I give him without Philibert's support? What would his future be like if I brought him back to the countryside to sweat and suffer like the other peasants? I told myself that with time, the hole in my heart would heal.

I was wrong. A short four months later, a youth knocked at our apartment door. "Are you Mademoiselle Baret?" he asked.

"Yes, I am." I gazed at him uncomprehending. "Can I help you?"

"Here," he said handing me a note. "I am to deliver this into your hands only."

I stared at him for several moments before I turned my eyes to the envelope. It was from the foundling home where I had left little Jean-Pierre. Gingerly, I pried it open. *"This is to inform you that your son, Jean-Pierre Baret, has died while in the care of the foster mother. He developed a fever, a sore throat, and difficulty breathing. He was called to the Lord in December."*

I closed the door and stumbled to the work bench where Philibert and I had been working. "I just received this notice from the foundling home. My little Jean-Pierre has died." My voice sounded far away, as if I was hearing someone at the end of a long tunnel.

I handed him the note. "What a shame. Such bad news for you," he said, as devoid of emotion as if he was commenting on a dinner invitation.

I stared at him in stunned silence. I let the note fall to the dining room table, turned and retreated to our bedroom. I closed the door, lay on the bed, sobbed into my pillow and did not reappear for the rest of the day.

Philibert did not disturb me until he came to bed. "Do you feel better now that you have the baby's death out of your system? Things will right themselves when you get back to work tomorrow."

I stared at him, stunned by his equanimity. Finally, I realized that his cold heart was as much a part of him as his love of plants. He was a self-important patrician whose sympathy did not extend beyond the end of his own arm. He would never change. But what were my choices? I could leave him, but where would I go? Or I could stay and resign myself to a life with a self-absorbed partner whose great passion did not extend to humanity. I tried to consoled myself with the knowledge that at least we had botany in common, and I had a place with him.

The next day, I left the bedroom and returned to my work. Hundreds of plants lay carefully arranged on tables filling the drawing room, sitting room, and kitchen. I reached out to touch the nearest plant, an inkberry holly - a winter evergreen, sent to us by the Jardin de Roi, on the day my baby died. I shook off my sorrow and prepared to resume my research with Philibert. Our routine remained the same, but my feelings toward him had shifted. I was twenty-four years old but as naïve as any young lover learning that her paramour is not the peerless gentleman she thought he was. So, I tucked my pain in the farthest corner of my heart and moved on.

* * *

"I'm home!" I tossed my light summer shawl on the settee and called when I returned from the market. Philibert did not respond. I listened for a reply but heard only a low groaning coming from the bedroom. I burst in and found Philibert on the bed curled into a fetal position.

"Philibert!" I called "What on earth is wrong?"

"My chest!" A spasm of coughing erupted almost choking him. When the coughing subsided, he breathed in short, gasping gulps.

"Philibert, what happened? Did this begin suddenly? I've never seen you like this before." I knelt next to the bed placing my hand on his forehead. Feeling no fever, I held his hands in both of mine.

"This has not happened for a long time," he panted. "When I was a child, I suffered attacks like this, but I outgrew them. I think it's the city, the air here. It . . ." He couldn't go on. Rasping coughs convulsed his body. "This is different. My chest . . . sharp, stabbing pain."

"Oh, Philibert! I will go to my notebook. It sounds like asthma, or . . ." I dared not even say it – tuberculosis. *No, not that! Please, not tuberculosis.*

I combed through the plants we brought from La Comelle, and the samples from the Jardin de Roi. When we arrived in Paris, I made it my habit to search the tables of the herb women in the market looking for plants to replace those I had left behind in La Comelle. I had rebuilt a respectable collection of medicinal herbs. I needed to find the right combination to stop the spasms, reduce the pain, then clear the lungs, and relax the muscles. It was a tall order with so many serious symptoms, but I went to work assembling my plant helpers: lavender, meadow sage, celandine to reduce the spasms; thyme, parsley, and ground ivy to clear his lungs; and an infusion of poppy petals and chamomile to help him sleep. He needed to sleep - the greatest healer of all.

When the crisis passed, he was exhausted and lay in bed for weeks recovering his strength. As adept as he was at botany, and despite having a medical degree, when a crisis hit, he was unable to help himself. If I had ever doubted it, now I knew he needed me after all. He improved slowly.

My household responsibilities in our Paris apartment multiplied. I continued making daily trips to the market, cooking, cleaning, stacking firewood, removing ashes from the hearth, hauling water up the stairs from the fountain in the square. Nonetheless, from his sick bed he instructed me in how I should care for the precious specimens from the Jardin de Roi, tending them as if they were our children.

"I'm ready to get up and sit in a chair," Philibert declared after two months of recouperation.

"Are you sure? Here, let me help you." I swung his legs over the edge of the bed and directed his slippered feet to the floor. He threw his arm over my shoulder, and I carefully slid him off the bed, supporting his weight as he swayed, trying to find his balance. His legs trembled under him, and he became dizzy. Philibert concentrated his attention on taking one wobbly step after another.

"You will be shaky for a while; you have been confined to bed for weeks. And the spasms have sapped your strength," I explained.

"But at last, I am upright, and ready to resume my life." He replied grinning, as proudly as a toddler taking his first steps. Optimism alone could not overcome his weakness. It would take months to regain his strength. But he was heading in the right direction, and his hopefulness revived us both.

One day, as I tended to our plant collection, with Philibert directing me from his over-stuffed chair, pointing this way and that like a concert master, a courier arrived at the door. He handed me a letter addressed to Philibert bearing the seal of Louis de Bougainville.

"What's this?" I handed the letter to Philibert. He went silent, holding the letter in his outstretched palm. I came to his side.

"It's from Louis de Bougainville, one of the most accomplished men of our time." I waited for him to offer more explanation.

"I understand. But why has he sent you a message?" I asked.

"He has updated the mathematics of calculus and is a member of both the French Académie des Sciences, and the Royal Society of London. He has had a distinguished career in the army and as an explorer." He looked at the seal on the unopened letter for a long time.

"Aren't you going to open it?" I looked over his shoulder as he broke the seal, and we read the missive together. It was from the French Minister of Marines.

"On the recommendation of the Academy of Sciences, Philibert Commerson is hereby appointed as the King's naturalist, to accompany Bougainville's expedition of circumnavigation. You are directed to draw up a report regarding observations on the natural history of the three kingdoms of Nature – animal, vegetable, and mineral, as well as physical as meteorological observations. Said voyage shall commence on or around November 1766 as weather and circumstance shall allow.

Shock and horror overwhelmed me. My heart sank and my knees buckled. My chest felt hollow as if I had been punched, and I could not take in breath. "Philibert what is the meaning of this? Did you know about this voyage?"

He stood mutely with his back to me holding the letter in his limp hand. If he had an explanation, he must tell me. Not giving an answer was tantamount to an admission of guilt.

"How long have you been conniving to take this voyage? Did you know about this appointment during your recovery? Is that what you and your friends from the Jardin discussed when you spent days the Jardin? Did you intend to just leave me behind? After everything we have been through together, after everything I have done for you – even making the ultimate sacrifice of giving up my son – even after nursing you through your illness, after all this, do you now plan to abandon me while you sail around the world?"

Finally, he stirred. "The directors at the Jardin du Roi have been discussing the possibility of sailing around the world for over a year. France is falling behind. The Netherlands, Spain, and Britain have already completed a circumnavigation and are busily claiming new lands for their countries. The king is determined to establish a French empire. My supporters put my name forward as chief naturalist. Voltaire, Queen Louisa Ulrika of Sweden, and Linnaeus himself have all provided references for me. How could I say no?"

I am not an emotionally weak woman. The strain of all that had happened over the past four years since dear Antoinette died suddenly became unbearable and I crumbled. The prospect of being left behind to fend for myself in a city I barely knew was the ultimate betrayal. I thudded onto the divan, wrapped my arms around knees and rocked back and forth. Hard as I tried, I could not stop the tears. Philibert did not speak but stood by silently as I recovered myself.

"When were you planning to tell me about this? To my knowledge women are not allowed on ships." My voice was hoarse and garbled. "This assignment means you must abandon me here in this city where I don't know a single soul and I do not belong."

"But you see Jeanne, the annual pay is generous and my stipend for expenses will be lavish. I would return a man of means, admired and respected. My professional future would be secure. And the prospect of adventure is irresistible. Just think I'd be botanizing in unknown climes around the world! It would change my life."

"Since my father died, I have been rootless, not quite belonging anywhere. I thought you and I were building a life together, that you were committed. You told me I would be with you forever, and here I am, facing my greatest fear again." I took several slow deep breaths, trying to steady myself while I chose my words carefully.

"A long sea voyage is dangerous. Men die, I may never see you again. What would I do without you? How would I support myself? Become a washer woman? Did you even once think about my welfare?" I softened my tone and changed my tack. "What would you do without me? Who would carry your equipment when you explore the world? Who would traipse across unknown landscapes behind you with plant presses, trowels, boxes, beakers, pens, and inks? Who would be as knowledgeable and capable as I? Just look around this place." I swept my arm over the extensive collection of plants arrayed over every surface. "Who else could do this?"

For Philibert, the idea of a botanical voyage of discovery shimmered like a mirage floating just beyond the horizon, and I knew he would not be able to resist its allure.

"I don't know. I hadn't thought of all that, but I will think of something." His shoulders sagged and the brilliance in his eyes faded. "We have about two months until the voyage launches to make a plan."

He moved toward me as if to embrace me, but I turned away and would not look at him. When I finally raised my eyes to meet his, it was not love that he saw, but shock, accusation, and terror.

"I will think of something. I promise," he said.

We did not speak of the matter again until several weeks later when he presented me with a document written on the finest parchment.

"Read it," he said. He stood facing me in a rather formal posture, with one hand tucked behind his back. He drew his hand forward and handed me an official-looking document rolled up and tied with a ribbon.

"What's this?" I wondered out loud.

"Read it," he said again, his eyes focused on the document. "You are right. Sea voyages can be dangerous. There are storms, hostilities between enemies, accidents. . . "

I gazed down at the parchment in my hand and unrolled it. I raised my head and found him staring intently at me.

So it began: *This is the last testament of Philibert Commerson. Being of sound mind. . . .*

"Go ahead. Read it."

Several paragraphs rolled on wherein he gave directions for the disposal of his body, his possessions and the plant collection we had labored over, if he should die at sea.

To Jeanne Baret, also known as Jeanne de Bonnefoy, my housekeeper, I leave monies to the total of six hundred livres to be paid in a single lump sum and any unpaid wages owed to her since September 6th, 1764, . . . In addition, I declare that all the linen, all the women's dresses and clothes in my Paris apartment are her own property, as well as all the furniture . . . If she chooses, she may stay in the apartment for one year after news of my death, which residence may provide time to organize the natural history specimens that are to be sent to the Royal Collection.

He had tried to give me the one thing I had lacked and longed for all my life. Security. All I could do was whisper "Thank you."

"It's my will," he explained. "If anything happens to me, the rent of this apartment will be paid for a full year. You will own everything here." He looked at me with hope.

"You would not leave me destitute. That, at least, is a comfort," I sighed. "Thank you."

I could not put my thoughts in order and did not trust myself to say the right thing. I could not untie the knot of emotions I felt - relief that he would see to my well-being if he died, anger that he would leave me for a better life without me, sadness that I would lose my lover and partner. I lit a tallow candle, took his hand, and led him to the bed. I perched behind him as his legs dangled over the edge, gently stroking his arms, and back, running my fingers through what remained of his curly black hair, now receding from his forehead. I felt his muscles relax and his breathing deepened. He turned toward me and gently pushed me down on the bed.

"Thank you, my love," he whispered. "I have come to realize I do not want to live without you, here or anywhere else. More than anything else, I want you to go with me," he said.

"I want to be with you too."

"There must be a way. We will think of something," he said as he covered me with his body. I cleared my mind of all other thoughts and gave myself wholly over to the intimacy of the moment.

"We will think of something. I know we will," I whispered.

CHAPTER SEVEN

L'ETOILE
FEBRUARY TO MARCH 1766

The coach was crowded, cold, and silent. Dismal winter weather dampened all conversation. Each passenger sank into his own thoughts. No one took note of me, masquerading as a young man bundled in my oversized great coat. The bindings meant to flatten my breasts were so tight I could hardly breathe. I squirmed, trying to find a comfortable position. The prosperous gentleman sitting next to me seemed not to notice me at all.

When we arrived at Rochefort, we wasted no time getting our baggage off-loaded onto the wide apron of beach that faced the port. Strewn over the muddy sand lay a welter of boxes, crates, barrels, and chests waiting for their owners to claim them. Nothing interrupted the view between the beach and the impossibly far horizon, only a vast expanse of rippling grey water shimmering in the sun. Ships large enough to hold my entire village bobbed at anchor in the deep water offshore, while smaller ships, fishing scows, and the tenders that carried passengers back and forth from the ships to the docks, crowded the shallow water nearer the docks.

Philibert found me standing amid the baggage, keeping an eye on our belongings. "What do you think? Are you ready?" he asked.

I ignored his question. It was unanswerable and irrelevant. How could I know if I was ready when I had no idea of how my life was about to change. We were going to board, whether I was ready or not.

"That one." I said, pointing to a huge, five-masted ship standing as tall as a three-story building. "Will we be sailing on that monster?"

"No. That vessel is a ship of the Line, a Navy warship. It is intended for battle. That ship over there," he said pointing to a sleek smaller vessel, "is a frigate. Captain Bougainville, the master of this voyage, is sailing a frigate. It is designed for speed and maneuverability, particularly useful for scouting shorelines. We will be skirting the shores of the lands we pass, occasionally mooring to explore new habitats and environments. I expect we will discover hundreds of new species. This is intended to be a voyage of discovery, after all, and Captain Bougainville is keen to claim new territories for France."

"Where is his ship?"

"He set sail last week and is already on his way to the Maldives as we speak. He will rejoin our ship when we reach Rio de Janeiro."

I had never heard of these places, much less envisioned sailing to them.

He pointed to a smaller, but still impressive vessel. "See that one, with three masts? Do you see how each sail is taller than the one in front of it? Look at the body shape. It is smaller and narrower with a long, pointed prow. It gives the ship a sleek appearance. Don't you agree?" I nodded wordlessly, and Philibert went on. "It's a schooner, also built for speed and maneuverability like the frigate, but it holds less cargo, so it can sail in shallower water. Pirates favor that one."

I shot a quick side-long glance at him. "Are you trying to scare me?"

Philibert chuckled. "Piracy is not as prevalent as it once was, but a ship known to be carrying riches back from the new world was still a target and had to be prepared to defend itself or out run the predators of the sea."

"Where is our ship?"

"Right there, my boy." He pointed to a smaller ship. "It has a shallow draft, and a flatter bottom. See how the body is bulbous at the water line, but narrows inward toward the rails? This gives it a larger cargo area." He watched me as I studied it. "That is the *L'Etoile*, the ship we will be sailing. Its mission on this voyage is to be a supply ship to Bougainville's frigate.

'*My Boy*.' That's how he addressed me. It brought me up cold. I was struggling to maintain my new persona as his valet. I must forget about Jeanne and become Jean. I hoped my costume - baggy pants held up with a wide waistband, a loose-fitting shirt, a bandana tied around my neck, topped by a knitted woolen cap - was ordinary enough among the deck hands to avoid unwanted attention. Abruptly, I became intensely aware of the pressure of the bindings flattening my breasts. *I'd better get used to it;* I thought. *I will need to bind my breasts every day until we complete our voyage, and who knows how long that will be.* It was incomprehensible to me that our route would take us around the entire globe. That would have been an exciting prospect if only I could stop thinking about the many ways our plans could go awry. But there was no backing out now.

I brought my attention back to the beach. "Are those guns I see?" I asked, pointing to the cannons protruding from port holes on two of the decks.

"Yes," he said, peering more closely at the ship's armament. "I can see eight-pounders in the open air on the quarter deck and twenty-six twelve-pounders on the fighting deck just below. It would be insane to sail without being able to defend ourselves. Even so, I don't expect we will need them."

Philibert turned away and walked a short distance down the beach. He did not want to be seen with me yet, as it would derail the plan we devised for getting me on board. Left alone, I could not resist the temptation to find someone to talk to. Dozens of questions beset my anxious mind. I shuffled over to a young man dressed as I was. I assumed he was looking for an opportunity to be taken on as a crewman on one of these ships. He leaned against a stack of sea trunks, watching the loading of the *L'Etoile*. I judged him to be no more than fourteen years old. He was fair-haired with a face more pretty than handsome, with the height of a fully grown man, but the narrow shoulders, and spindly arms and legs of someone who has not quite grown into his own skin.

"You're not loading the ship," I said.

"No, I'm hanging back. I have already secured a job and it's not doing menial labor like loading the ship. They hire stevedores for that."

I was impressed by his confidence. "What is your position?"

He looked at me suspiciously, but apparently concluded I was a landlubber, not a spy for the boatswain, who might punish him for slacking. He evaded my question. "Is this your first voyage?" he replied.

"Yes, it is, and I must admit I'm a bit apprehensive."

"And well you should be. I have been apprenticed to the timekeeper since I was twelve and have made several voyages. I can tell you I have been terrified many times. I'm savoring my last few minutes on land," he shrugged trying to appear casual and calm, but I guessed he was almost as apprehensive as I was. "Is this your first voyage?"

"Yes, my first voyage. I am assistant to Monsieur Commerson, the ship's naturalist. Of what use is a timekeeper on a voyage?" I asked, betraying my ignorance.

"The day at sea is divided into six watches, each four hours long. The timekeeper keeps track of the time so the officers can estimate how far we have sailed. We use a thirty-minute sandglass. We turn the glass every half hour when the sands have run through. Then we strike the bell, using one stroke for each half hour of our watch. Two strikes of the bell equal one hour. You'll soon get the gist of it."

"It sounds like a very important job."

"Yes, it is." his adolescent body swelled a little with pride. Then he returned his eyes to the barrels, kegs, and chests being hauled up the gangway. "They are stowing everything we will need to live for many months – dried meat, beer, bread, cheeses, dried peas, oatmeal, hard biscuits and fresh water. We will need plenty as there over are over a hundred men on *L'Etoile*, and this will be a long voyage."

Together we watched the men prod the live cargo - cows, goats, and chickens - all of them objecting loudly, up the gangway and into the hold. I hated to imagine their misery in the dark depths of the lowest deck of the ship awaiting the day when they would grace the dinner plates of the sailors.

"You seem to know a lot about the workings of a ship. I am Jean, what is your name?"

"You are a curious one, aren't you." He looked me over again. "And you look like a complete novice," he chuckled, hawked up a wad of spittle and spit it at my feet. A churlish habit, I thought, for a boy so young. But I had a lot to learn about the habits of sailors.

I ignored the implied insult. "You're right. I know more about how to cater to the needs of my employer than I do about seafaring."

"My name is Etienne," he replied. Etienne scanned me top to toe once more. He cocked his head to the side like a confused dog and shrugged. "I'll see you on board," he said. He brought two fingers to his cap, nodding slightly, and sauntered away.

I loitered on the beach, waiting for the agreed-upon sign from Philibert indicating I should join him. A man dressed in an elaborately decorated dark blue coat with ornately embroidered cuffs and a sword in a white scabbard hanging from his belt hurried toward Philibert, who was standing on the beach among our belongings. He grasped Philibert's hand in a hearty handshake. His self-assured stride and stiff, upright military bearing marked him as a navy officer. He wore his greying hair short and swept back and he sported a well-trimmed goatee.

"You are Philibert Commerson, I assume? Let me introduce myself. I am François de la Giraudais, commanding officer of *L'Etoile*. I was told to look for you." For some moments he stared at our extensive assortment of field equipment piled in an untidy heap.

"That's quite a lot of gear you have. I didn't realize a botanist would need much more than a shovel and a heavy book in which to press plants."

"Oh yes, we have an abundance of tools of the trade." Philibert puffed out his chest and used his most officious tone.

The captain stroked his goatee thoughtfully and looked vaguely back and forth between the ship and our heap of paraphernalia. He gestured toward the *L'Etoile*, already riding low in the water, heavy with cargo.

Giraudais began again. "I am pleased to make your acquaintance." His words were friendly, but he looked dubious. "I wish you good fortune in your scientific mission. It will be a long voyage, and we will have plenty of opportunity to get to know each other better."

"Yes, no doubt," Philibert responded. "I look forward to sailing under your capable leadership."

When their introductory pleasantries were done, Philibert pulled a silk handkerchief from his pocket, and waved it in the air before wiping his brow. That was my signal. I sauntered toward him, my shoulders slouched, hands stuffed into the pockets of my baggy pants, shuffling my feet, with my over-large cap pulled low over my brow. The captain's eyes rested on me, for an uncomfortably long moment. A flicker of confusion sparked in his eyes, then quickly vanished. *Oh no*, I thought, *has he already recognized me for what I am - a girl?* He turned away from me and returned his attention to Philibert.

"Hey there, boy!" Philibert summoned me to his side, and I ambled toward him. "I need you to load my equipment onto the ship. It's expensive and would be impossible to replace on the voyage, so be very careful. Please attend to that right away."

"No need for that," the captain said. "We have stevedores for that."

"I appreciate the offer, sir, but my equipment is fragile and requires special care. This boy will do fine."

The captain looked skeptically at my slim frame and uncalloused hands. Most sailors were coarse, brawny men capable of slinging one heavy barrel over each shoulder and hauling them up the gangway without breaking a sweat.

Addressing the captain's skepticism, Philibert explained. "At the last minute I found myself without a field assistant. Just last week, my nephew who was meant to accompany me, declined the opportunity. I urgently needed someone to handle my equipment. I met this youth a few days ago on the coach from Paris. I questioned him extensively. He was heading toward Port de Tonnay-Charente hoping to find work at the docks. He had no commitments. He is moderately educated. He tells me his mother was an herb lady before her death, so he claims to have some botanical knowledge, meager though it may be. I asked him if he would accompany me as my servant, and he agreed." Philibert followed the captain's wary gaze as he considered me more carefully. "He looks scrawny, I know," Philibert apologized, reading the captain's expression. "But he has assured me he can haul my gear."

I made a show of looking the ship over as if I was a keen judge of sailing vessels. "Yes sir, I can do that." I spoke softly in a low register and hoped it would suffice. I was a boy after all, not a man.

"Can you have one of your men direct my boy to our quarters?"

Captain Giraudais surveyed our belongings once more and stroked his beard. "Monsieur Commerson, do you intend to keep all this equipment in your quarters?"

"Yes, I do. I will need it close at hand to conduct my botanical investigations when we stop along the way. It would not do to have it buried in the hold."

"In that case, the cabin I arranged for you will be far too small to accommodate your equipment. You may take my cabin, and I will occupy the smaller cabin I had intended for you."

"Sir, that is more than generous of you, but I do not wish to inconvenience you in any way."

"Please, Monsieur Commerson, it is no inconvenience for me. I will move to the First Mate's quarters. It will afford me the advantage of being closer to my men, therefore more able to discern discontent before it spreads. The sleeping quarters on long voyages like ours are a breeding ground for vexation. Since you with all your belongings will need larger quarters, it will be mutually beneficial for us to trade cabins." The captain brought his fingers to the brim of his tricorn hat, and with a nod, turned to go. As he left, he motioned to one of his crewmen. "Help this man and his servant take their belongings to my cabin." Then, looking back toward Philibert he said, "We can find an unoccupied hammock for your boy below decks with the rest of the hands."

I shot a wide-eyed glance at Philibert, silently pleading with him to explain to the captain why this arrangement was unacceptable. How could I sleep among the rabble of sailors? He avoided my eyes, shrugged his shoulders and boarded. We followed the crewman down a short flight of stairs to the captain's quarters. The crewman shouldered our sea chests, and I gripped an armful of heavy plant presses and followed them to our quarters.

The captain's cabin was located on the gun deck below the main deck at the rear of the ship. At first glance, it looked small, but it was so efficiently arranged that there was a cranny or corner for every purpose. A pair of windows equipped with wide sills looked out over the riffling grey water of the harbor. On the sill sat an hourglass, a compass, and a small spyglass. A glass-doored cabinet with several shelves hung above a capacious sea chest, a perfect place to store the smaller tools of our trade - glass vials for seeds, tiny boxes for insects, magnifying glasses, and tweezers. The cabin had two quarter galleries, one for sleeping and one set up as a latrine. A comfortable bed like a hammock with rigid, coffin-like sides hung and from the ceiling. Next to it, on a sturdy six-drawered dresser, sat a heavily weighted wash basin and ewer. The chief luxury this cabin offered was the private latrine tucked into a corner at the far end of the room enclosed within a heavy sailcloth partition. The ordinary deck hands and servants used privies perched over the open water at the bow of the ship. I had never considered the details of relieving myself aboard a ship filled with a hundred men. The complications of passing as a boy were becoming clear.

"You can stack the equipment on the floor next to the table," Philibert directed me imperiously.

When the equipment was stowed, I turned on Philibert and squawked at him. "You can't seriously expect me to bunk in with the men!" I hissed. "Why didn't you speak up for me?"

Philibert spun around and confronted me. "What was I supposed to say? '*No, my boy is really a girl and can't sleep alongside the men*'? We need your disguise to be unquestioned. Singling you out for special treatment would attract attention and start tongues wagging. Let me remind you the reason for your disguise in the first place is that women are not allowed on ships. The captain would suffer serious repercussions if it were known he allowed a woman on board. And my reputation would be ruined. Heaven only knows what the captain would do to you."

"But this is not right! Look at those men! Did you see the unwashed, riffraff that swarmed the deck when we were loading? They are an unsavory assortment of slovenly ne'er do wells decked out in dirty, threadbare, clothing. You're dreaming if you think they will treat me kindly. I will be a sheep among wolves."

Philibert ignored my distress. "You can stack our equipment on the floor next to the table. Now is not the time to start asking for special treatment."

I seethed, like a pot of tiny bubbles on the verge of bursting into a full boil. I would need to find an excuse, a plausible reason why it was imperative to share Philibert's quarters. But for now, I did as I was told and stowed our belongings in the quarter gallery adjacent to Philibert's quarters. I found spaces on the table facing the window for the vasculum, a cylindrical tube with a shoulder strap to hold delicate specimens without crushing them, plant presses, magnifying glasses, a small microscope, trowels, picks, brushes, pens, pencils and many sheets of linen rag paper.

"This will do nicely." Philibert smiled as he slumped into his hanging bed.

"I'm telling you, Philibert, I would sooner spend the night in the hold with the cargo than in the hammocks with those uncouth sailors."

"We must do as the captain orders. In his eyes you are just a servant boy, and we need him to continue believing that."

"In that case, I will need to protect myself. You brought two pistols, didn't you?"

Philibert nodded, carefully loaded one of the pistols and handed it to me without objection. I lingered on deck watching the dark water swallow the dying sun.

CHAPTER EIGHT

AN UNEASY FIT
1767

On the morning of February first, 1767, *L'Etoile*, launched into heavy grey fog that hung low above the waters of the Rochefort harbor. I wasn't wrong in my assessment of the sailors' sentiments about me. From the first day, they made their suspicions clear with their skeptical glances and rough guffaws when I passed by. I ignored them as best I could, but I couldn't eliminate all interactions with the men. Undercurrents of hostility hung in the wind like an unfurled sail.

They watched me take liberties afforded to none of the other servants. I was allowed to walk openly on the main deck with Philibert. I came and went from his cabin at will, using the latrine in his quarters, not relieving myself over the rail or at the heads in the prow of the ship. They were immediately suspicious that Philibert and I had a relationship that was closer than just that of master and servant.

On the first night, hoping to be less obtrusive, I waited until darkness shrouded sailors' quarters. I bedded down in my hammock, as tired as I had ever been. My breasts ached and burned under their bindings. More than anything else, I needed rest. Within minutes I heard shuffling boots and the snorts of barely suppressed laughter coming toward me. The hackles rose on my neck and my blood ran cold. Then I felt a hand grip the edge of my hammock. I stayed as still as sleeping cat, opened one eye, and pointed the gun between the eyes of the closest man.

"If you take one step closer, I will blow your head off." I used my lowest, gravelliest voice. "I am not joking. This gun is loaded, and I know how to use it. I propped myself up on one elbow facing them. In the darkness, with my sailor's cap pulled low, shrouding my face, I slowly pointed the gun at each one of them in turn. "Who wants to be the first? Who wants to test me?"

They backed away slowly. "Get back to your hammocks and don't bother me again."

Growling and muttering, they retreated, but I had no illusions that this would be the last of my troubles with them. As much as I wanted to race to the safety of Philibert's cabin, I dared not look like a child hiding behind his mother's apron strings. I laid awake throughout the night, as still as sand on a windless beach. When morning came, I left that hammock intending never to go back.

"You were right about sleeping with the sailors," Philibert said after hearing the story of my terrifying night. "I will talk to the captain."

The story of how the sailors attempted to interfere with me spread among the crew as fast as a lightning bolt igniting tinder. Before the sun had cleared the horizon, Captain Giraudais had already heard what happened the night before. This was a dangerous situation for him. He risked humiliation, even loss of command if his superiors believed he had knowingly allowed a woman on board. Before the day was out, he called me to account for the incident, assuming I had somehow incited the men's behavior.

Standing before him in the officer's wardroom, my entire body quivered with fear, nausea gorged my throat, and exhaustion from a lost night's sleep fogged my brain. But I needed to show a brave front as I had with the sailors last night.

"What do you have to say for yourself, Jean Baret?" He hadn't taken much notice of me previously. He saw me only as Philibert's young assistant, youthful, gangly, and still beardless. But now he scrutinized every inch of my body. "That is your name, isn't it? Who are you? You say you are a youth, but clearly the crewmen believe you are lying."

I hadn't thought I would have to explain my irregular behavior and appearance so soon, but I needed a plausible story right here, right now. I took a deep breath and spoke, hoping to be convincing.

"Yes, I understand. I want you to know I did nothing to incite the men. My father was a merchant and trader," I began. "When I reached twelve years of age, he took me with him on a trading mission between Marseille and Izmir, Turkey, hoping he could train me to the trade. Turkish pirates raided our ship, my father was killed, and I was taken prisoner. Do you know what Turks do with captured boys before they become men? The last thing I remember was one of the Turks holding a blade to my throat while another man pulled him away from me, gesticulating toward my underdeveloped private parts and laughing like a hyena. When he brought the blade to my crotch I lost consciousness. I was lucky I survived the mutilation. My hopes of living a normal life as a man died that day."

The captain sat in silence for a long time. The Turks were well known for their brutality, and European seamen heard many colorful tales of youths who were deliberately emasculated so they could guard the harems without danger of sexual contact with the women. Their bodies would grow strong, but they often remained beardless with high-pitched voices. He did not ask for further details. His eyes remained opaque, guarding his own thoughts. The story sounded plausible, if not totally convincing, but Philibert's scientific mission was too prestigious and important to be cancelled. He had been appointed by the King, after all. Besides, it was too late for Philibert to find a new botanical assistant.

"Gather your belongings and move them to Commerson's quarters. I will arrange a hammock to be installed for you there. Make yourself scarce. Don't strike up any conversations with the men. Now, go. I do not want you disrupting this voyage again, or I'll throw you overboard."

I tried mightily to remain unobtrusive, but I could not disappear completely from the eyes of the men. Many of the sailors ignored me, immersed in their own responsibilities. Others, like dangerously vindictive children, despised me and subjected me to small aggressions, knocking me against the rail when they passed, or extending a foot to trip me as I carried a food tray to Philibert. Clearly, I was not welcome among them. To all outward appearances everything remained calm, but jealousy and ill-will swam beneath the surface, showing only a hint of itself, like a shark's fin cleaving the water.

Philibert's air of superiority with the ship's crew did nothing to endear him either, he was almost as unpopular as I was. The captain would have loved to replace me as Philibert's assistant and demote me to a more menial job. But much to his chagrin, there were no candidates qualified for the job. Most of the crewmen were illiterate and ignorant of the natural world. There were, however, a few other scientists and a small coterie of gentlemen aboard he hoped could take my place.

In addition to the officers, there were men with important skills. Antoine Veron, for example, a mathematician and ship's astronomer, was fully involved with his own important, possibly ground-breaking research determining longitude while at sea. How could the captain tell Charles de Romainville, the cartographer and engineer, that he should follow a botanist around in search of new plants. Francois Vives, the ship's surgeon, was on call day and night tending to the medical needs of the crew.

Then Giraudais's eyes fell on Charles-Nicolas Othon, Prince of Nassau-Siegen, a member of the German royalty. Judging by his extravagant wardrobe, it was hard to envision him tramping about in the wild places Philibert would be exploring. I had seen aristocratic men with elegant clothing before, but nothing I had ever seen compared with the prince's velvet breeches, colorfully embroidered waistcoats, delicate lacey ascots, long full-skirted coats, and his perfectly coifed wig. His mincing steps added to the impression of an elegant lady. He was a very good-humored young man, adventurous, with a cheerful disposition. But even if he had been interested, there was no chance someone of his elevated position could work in service to Philibert. It would be an unpardonable breach of protocol. That left only me to serve the botanist's needs. As much as he would have liked to replace me, Giraudais found no one else to serve as both Commerson's personal servant and botanical assistant.

The scientists and aristocrats on the voyage sought out each other's company, exchanging stories and sharing information. Philibert, proud of his own professional reputation, was well-respected, though not always well-liked, by the other scientists and notables with one exception. The ship's doctor, Francois Vives, despised him. Unlike Philibert, whose personal wealth and professional reputation allowed him to abandon the practice of medicine in favor of botany, Vives, with his proletarian background, was bound to work mainly below decks tending to the medical needs of the sailors.

From the very first day, Vives made it his mission to undermine my status as Philibert's assistant, and he never missed an opportunity to goad me with suggestive gestures, snide remarks, and sly implications. He made it perfectly clear that he did not, for one moment, believe I was a boy. He circulated rumors among the crew that Philibert and I were guilty of either sodomy or lying to the captain. Worst of all, he subtly circulated the rumor that there was a woman on board dressed as a man. Though he didn't specifically name me, he planted the seed of doubt, and many believed that I was a dangerous imposter who would bring bad luck to the voyage. I was trapped and could not escape my situation, so I resolved to carry on in the most impeccable manner possible, giving no one a reason to call my behavior into question. The last thing I wanted was to give anyone reason to fault me.

For the first two months of our voyage, we sailed on calm seas. Little did I realize that I was about to be swallowed by the dangerous undercurrent created by Vives.

CHAPTER NINE

CROSSING THE LINE
MARCH TO APRIL 1767

The morning of March twenty-first dawned calm and clear. *L'Etoile* rocked on an azure sea, her half-filled sails propelling her at a stately pace over the Atlantic Ocean. After almost two months without seeing land or another vessel, *L'Etoile* had become a universe unto itself with its own rules, customs, and superstitions. The crewmen repeated their tasks day after day, over and over, keeping within the grooves of their well-worn ruts.

L'Etoile's crew numbered 103 men, and the *Boudeuse,* Captain Bougainville's ship, had more than 300. Both ships conformed to highly regimented routines and peace among the crew was thereby maintained. Although ours was intended to be a voyage of discovery, the captains were military men who maintained tight discipline and their crews adhered to a strict schedule.

After meeting the watchman's assistant during the loading, I was curious about the time-keeper's job. The task seemed simple, but Etienne had spoken with pride about his apprenticeship, so I asked

Philibert to tell me more. "I met a young man on shore who was the timekeeper's apprentice, and he seemed quite proud of himself. Now I can see why. But he was so young."

"That's no surprise, many boys and young men work on ships. Some follow in their father's footsteps, some are running away from bad circumstances, some are simply adventurous. You'll see. They will all find out soon enough that life aboard a ship is demanding and dangerous."

"That's exactly what he said."

Philibert's mouth twisted into a rakish grin. "You, and the other neophyte crewmen will soon find out that sailing includes all kinds of unexpected experiences."

* * *

As we approached the latitude where we left the northern hemisphere and entered the southern hemisphere, the atmosphere onboard changed. Suddenly, a lively, festive mood overtook the crew. In the seaman's quarters, among the hammocks, the men formed small cabals to work on bizarre costumes. I didn't know what to make of it, and despite my questions, Philibert made only vague references to the ritual of 'crossing the line.' There was no one else I could ask, but I grew wary and vigilant, skeptical of all the excitement.

On the morning of March twenty-eighth, Philibert informed me that today would be a very special day, but he was cagey and ambiguous about the reason. "Today, you must stay on deck. There will be an important ceremony meant to appease Neptune, the God of the Sea. The sailors have been working on their costumes for weeks. It's all in good fun, though the proceedings can get a bit rowdy."

His words neither reassured me nor explained the nature of this ceremony. The hair on the back of my neck rose as when a bow is dragged over the strings of a badly tuned violin.

Early in the morning, all hands were called on deck. The younger sailors, painted top to toe in a hideous green color, scrambled up the rigging, swinging like monkeys from the ratlines that formed the rope ladders for accessing the sails to the dizzying heights of the crow's nest. Those on deck had fashioned crude 'skirts' from lengths of frayed rope, donned wigs made from mops, and sported upside-down cooking pans on their heads. All the men had ginned up one ridiculous costume or another.

On deck, one man, dressed in a flowing 'gown' made of sail cloth played the part of Salacia, Neptune's consort, and goddess of the sea. Attended by her 'ladies in waiting,' she ceremoniously delivered a letter to Captain Giraudais who read it in a booming voice loud enough to be heard over the din:

Hear ye, hear ye. The following is a missive from King Neptune.

King Neptune, Lord of the Seas, protector of the watery realms, and defender of the depths, demands that all who enter his southern realm submit an offering to appease his pride and prove his absolute dominion over the seas.

Let it be known that all the scallywags, neophytes who know not of his glorious realm, and wishing to cross the great line that divides North from South for the first time must prove themselves worthy by enduring an initiation.

Only those who sacrifice themselves to the Great Sea God will be deemed worthy. Only those who have endured the ritual baptism will be permitted to cross the line. Prepare yourselves. King Neptune is coming.

I looked from one face to another searching for a clue to the meaning of this baffling 'baptism." High-spiritedness became chaos as sailors who had previously endured the ritual of 'crossing the line' smeared their faces with soot and festooned themselves with feathers glued to their green-painted bodies. The experienced sailors swung wildly from the rigging screeching out a cacophony of animal calls - cackling, hooting, barking, and neighing. Howls of laughter split the air as the crewmen elbowed each other displaying their most lascivious gestures.

After the letter was read, King Neptune assumed his "throne," an overturned bucket. Neptune's crown already tilted upon his head making him look decidedly less than regal. I was among the scallywags, the other first-time crossers, who formed a milling crowd in front of Neptune's throne.

"I command you to make an oath to me and all the gods of the sea that you will never commit adultery with the wives of your shipmates. Do you so swear?"

The crewmen hooted and guffawed, taunting us scallywags. We mumbled and shuffled our feet, glancing nervously. We were hundreds of miles from anyone's wife, so all the men called out "We so swear." The crowd erupted into guffaws. Many eyes turned toward me, fingers pointing, and elbows nudging.

Using tightly twisted wet towels, pots, pans, mops, belts or anything else that came to hand, the crewmen ran us scallywags through a disorganized gauntlet, flailing away at us, pulling, pushing, poking and prodding until we stood at the railing of the ship. Knowing what was coming, the other neophytes removed their shirts and hats readying themselves to endure the ritual. I, of course, was clueless about what was about to happen and could not risk taking my shirt off. I remained fully clothed, which made me an even more obvious target for hazing. Filthy hands reached out at me from all directions, snatching at my clothes. If I had been apprehensive before, I was now terrified. After we took our oath to Neptune, the crew manhandled us to the ship's rail. The scallywags' good-natured smiles disappeared when we all looked over the edge. A jerry-rigged "bathtub"– a sail cloth floating in a submerged lifeboat - forming a pool floated next to the ship.

"This way, lads," a crewman called as he slithered down ropes tethering ship to the 'bathtub' bobbing in the water below. Soon there were several crewmen paddling in the floating pool. Their laughing faces turned upward toward the horrified scallywags peering down from the rail. Some struggled to run back to safety. Most of us, including me, could not swim and what had been a good-natured celebration suddenly looked like a life-threatening nightmare.

Anxiety choked me, my heart pounded so hard I could hear it in my ears, and with the bindings suffocating me, I could barely breathe.

"What's the problem?" a laughing crewman shouted. "Are you cowards? Come on now, down you go." With this, the scallywags on *L'Etoile* were surrounded by sailors on deck, and either voluntarily jumped into the pool or were pushed over the edge. I stood, paralyzed, until someone gave me a mighty shove. I screamed in a decidedly unmanly voice. The "pool" turned out to be a veritable cesspool of fetid water, fouled by the contents of the livestock pens, rotten food scraps, and every form of detritus that could be found on deck. There was no escape. As I flailed and gasped, desperate not to swallow the horrid swill, strong sailors in the pool pulled me under. Their hands grabbed at my body, tore at my clothes, and smeared soot over my face as I hopelessly struggled to climb the rope back up to the deck. I thrashed, as I tried to defend myself, biting, scratching, twisting and turning to escape the groping hands of the men who pulled me under over and over again until I was sure this would be my last day on earth.

By the time I clawed my way back onboard, my bindings were shredded to ribbons, but still loosely bound around me. I retreated to our cabin, bruises already blossoming over my entire body, blood dripping from my nose, scratches and abrasions scoring my skin. My clothing was unspeakably filthy. I sat numbly on the edge of my cot trying to collect myself but panic still gripped me. As my heartbeat slowed the pain of my abrasions and lacerations emerged. There was nothing I could do but clean myself and my clothes and tend to my injuries. When Philibert entered the cabin chuckling, and began to make light of my humiliation, I erupted like Vesuvius.

"How dare you pretend this so-called "baptism" was all in fun. Do I look like I had fun?" I stood eye to eye with him, my hands on my hips, and spat at his feet. "You made absolutely no attempt to help me. You didn't even warn me what was in store. How would you like it if I abandoned you in your hour of need? I have never let you down. I have always been there for you, providing every comfort my skills allowed. And this is how you repay my devoted service? By subjecting me to this travesty you call a 'baptism?'"

Philibert stood in silence as anger and shame flamed over his face. I could see he felt bad about the indignity I'd suffered, but he resented being blamed for the fiasco. He said nothing, and I had nothing more to say either. For weeks Philibert and I barely spoke to each other.

The miles of sea that followed were among the worst of the entire trip. For weeks we sailed through an oceanic desert with nothing of interest to study. Even the fish shunned us. There were no scattered islands to explore, nothing but an empty, sullen sea, jealously hiding its secrets. Aside from a single tuna the men caught, there was nothing to relieve the tedium of the ship's routine.

My skin erupted in scaly, itchy blisters beneath my bindings. I was discouraged, disheartened, and despondent. Philibert had disappointed me in so many ways I could hardly speak to him. For his part, he never completely overcame his seasickness, and his leg wound refused to heal. The skin around the injury, which was originally red, turned purple then black. Intermittently it bled and released a dirty-looking, foul-smelling discharge. He finally had to beg me to treat his never-healing lesion. I could not let his injury become gangrenous, so I relented. I prepared compresses soaked in tincture of echinacea immersed in aromatic wine. I didn't have much hope this would cure the wound, but at least it could prevent it from getting worse. Regardless of how my feelings for Philibert had changed, I had no choice but to make peace and tend to him.

CHAPTER TEN

MONTEVIDEO TO RIO DE JANIERO
AND BACK AGAIN
APRIL TO NOV 1767

On April eighteenth, the barrelman manning the crow's nest cried "Land Ho!" Relief coursed through me. The cloud that had hung over me since the humiliation of crossing the line finally evaporated and my self-inflicted prison sentence of dread and loathing ended.

After three months at sea, confined with over a hundred men on this small ship, the cry incited a flurry of activity as frenzied as a hive of bothered bees. Within moments, the first mate and the navigator flanked Captain Giraudais on the quarter deck as he squinted through his spyglass.

"It's Cape Frio" the navigator explained. I wasn't supposed to be on deck without Philibert, but I had taken to escaping the confines of our cabin and secreting myself in an unobtrusive hiding place among the bales, boxes, and chests where I could observe the ship's activities and overhear conversations on the open deck. So far, I had not been discovered.

"From this point, we enter the waters off Rio de Janeiro," Giraudais explained to the officers, scientists, and gentlemen gathered on the deck. "But we will not be anchoring. Our instructions are to wait off the coast of Montevideo until we receive further orders from Captain Bougainville. When he gives the command, we will sail back up to Rio de Janeiro to meet him."

Giraudais lowered his spyglass. His expression became stoney and solemn. "I want you to know that I have surveyed the hold, and I am aware that you have packed it full of trinkets and rummage rather than supplies. If we had to survive on the food down there now, we would all starve to death in a few short months. Thus far, I have turned a blind eye to this wicked foolishness because I was confident we could resupply when we reached port. Captain Bougainville will not be lenient when he inspects the ship and sees how the space has been squandered on useless baubles, rather than the food and water we will need for our onward journey. I will allow you to disembark in Montevideo and you will dispose of these useless items immediately. They must be gone and replaced with needed supplies by the time Captain Bougainville joins us."

I couldn't believe my ears. Captain Giraudais just admitted he had known about this transgression since the beginning of the voyage. He must have considered what would happen if we didn't have enough supplies because the space meant for necessities had been squandered on useless contraband that served no purpose except to line the pockets of the crew. Despite their knowledge of the risks, the temptation to make a few extra francs overrode good sense.

When I brought the matter up with Philibert, he characteristically dismissed my concerns. "Don't worry. Sailors have been doing this for hundreds of years. It's just an opportunity to make a little extra money. Everyone does it. The captain himself is not blameless. Like the others, he too expects to make a tidy profit. We will sell our trade goods in Montevideo and then resupply. No need to fret."

I lifted one skeptical eyebrow but held my peace. To the best of my limited knowledge the journey between Montevideo through the Straits of Magellan, then on to the Pacific, would take many months. I hadn't studied geography, but I had seen Philibert's globe, and I knew that Montevideo was in the tropics where food was plentiful, and the Straits of Magellan were at the bottom of the world in a land of ice and snow. How could we gather supplies at the bottom of the world? And after we passed through the straits, we would enter the Pacific Ocean, an almost endless expanse of water. The vast Pacific was littered with tiny, scattered islands and finding one of them with enough food to fill our hold would be like finding the proverbial needle in the haystack. I had no idea how long such a voyage would take, but there must be some plan to restock enough food to feed us for the duration. There had to be!

A bright sun was burning through the morning mist as Montevideo loomed into view. Aside from the usual disarray, garbage, dingey saloons and bawdy houses near the docks, as was common in most ports, the town seemed to be neatly laid out. Montevideo was a rather new town. Its buildings had not yet sullied by the destructive forces of time, weather, and hard use. An imposing citadel sat atop a hill overlooking a city of white stucco, red-roofed buildings, and a large cathedral loomed over the town center.

In the days after we anchored, the crew scurried between the ship and the town with armfuls of trinkets, selling the contraband as quickly as possible, and turning their goods into cash. I was under no illusions about how the money would be spent. By now, I understood the workings of a sailor's mind and was aware of the recreations a harbor town offered men starved for female companionship. That night, I watched from my sheltered niche on the deck as the men stumbled back to the ship from a riotous evening bingeing on liquor and prostitutes. Before long, they had squandered all the money they gained by wasting cargo space for the sake of cheap trifles instead of food and water.

The next morning, Philibert summoned me. "Come with me to the hold and bring a large sack." I followed him down the ladder, perplexed by the amount of empty space left after the trinkets had been removed. Philibert grabbed arms full of trifles and stuffed them in the sack.

"You brought this frippery just like the sailors?" I was appalled by his bad judgment.

"Well, yes. A surgeon friend of mine asked me to handle these goods for him. I could see no reason to overlook an opportunity to earn a little profit."

"How long will the rest of this voyage take?"

"No one really knows. Magellan's first circumnavigation took three years. There have been several others of varying lengths since then. To the best of my knowledge, it should take between two and three years." He looked at me, mildly irritated. "I know you are fretting but there is no need. Provisioning the ship is not our concern. Captain Giraudais will see to it. Our job is to discover new flora and fauna and expand scientific knowledge. Now that we are here, we have an opportunity to finally leave the ship and fulfill our purpose on this voyage."

The city of Montevideo was the only blot on the pristine landscape. Beyond the town's boundaries the evidence of human activity disappeared quickly. Set apart on its jutting peninsula, it nestled against a luxurious profusion of exotic plants. Impenetrable emerald-green forests, dotted with marshes, and wetlands ringed the coast creating a spectacle of tremendous abundance. *This is what Eden must have looked like,* I thought.

As soon as the nonsense with the contraband was finished, we boarded one of the tenders that plied the short distance from the anchored ship to the shore. Once there, we splashed into the shallows and slogged to the beach. I closed my eyes, threw my head back and inhaled deeply and dug my toes into the soft white sand. Liberated from the crowded confines of the ship for the first time in months, I felt as free as a dog let off its leash. My identity as a young man went unchallenged and the people bustling around the shore ignored me. When I walked the streets, not a single disapproving cluck or skeptical eye was cast my way. I was blessedly anonymous and totally unremarkable. Though my bindings still chafed and itched in the stifling equatorial heat, there was a distinct advantage in being perceived as a boy. I could stride along, swinging my arms, looking others straight in the eye, rubbing elbows with the crowd and no one gave me a second look.

For twenty idyllic days we explored Montevideo's surroundings. Despite the captain's order not to venture beyond town, Philibert was determined to do what he was hired to do – explore for new plants and brazenly ignored those orders.

Fresh air, redolent with the scent of flowers and trees, replaced the sour, ever-present smell of vinegar used to clean the ship's decks and tar that staunched its leaks. I allowed memories of the difficulties of the voyage to sink into the sea like an untethered anchor. Montevideo beckoned.

Aside from seeing a few sharks, a tuna and leaping porpoises, during the two-month passage from Rochefort, the voyage had been punctuated only by Philibert's persistent seasickness and his suppurating wound. I had plenty of time to grow nostalgic for long afternoons among the fields and forests of La Comelle.

Along the way *L'Etoile* had been tossed about by violent weather, ferocious winds, and mountainous waves. It was a wonder our small ship survived. The idyllic terrain around Montevideo was our reward.

I worked as hard as three men. With only a few precious weeks in Montevideo, I was impatient to get started. Beaches, dunes, shorelines, coastal wetlands, lagoons and the magnificent tropical rainforest beckoned. With the *L'Etoile* anchored close to land, we wasted no time arranging a small pirogue to carry us along the water's edge each day. The pilots, two tall, muscular negroes, knew the shoreline, its inlets, tiny islands, and rocky spits intimately. Their knowledge allowed us to pause wherever we wanted for however long we desired. We knew at once that this place would be a treasure trove of new species.

"Look at all this!" Philibert swept his outstretched arm in a wide arc across the landscape. "This is why the King selected me to make this voyage. He knows, with my skills, I will glean a wealth of knowledge and return to Paris as France's most eminent, well-respected botanist." His pridefulness and pomposity revolted me, even though I knew he was, in fact, well respected and knowledgeable. I simply nodded in reply.

Heat glistened on my upper lip and rivulets of sweat slid down my back as intense heat enveloped me in its torrid cocoon. The humidity bore down on me like dead weight. The world changed the instant we crossed from the sunny beach to the shadowy forest. Slender shards of light like daggers pierced the gloom below the dense canopy. What the rainforest subtracted in visibility it gave back in a mélange of discordant sounds. Every insect, bird, frog, and mammal buzzed, called, croaked or howled, raining noise down on us like a torrential deluge.

There are not enough words in our language to describe the shades of green we saw. To say the foliage was abundant is like saying water is wet. Mosses, ferns, vines, statuesque palm trees, and all manner of unique shrubs, each had its own shade of green. The calls of extravagantly colorful birds filled the air with a symphony of sound as they flashed through the dense forest.

Every day, we rose early, eager for the day's adventures. I packed the food and equipment we would need for the day - a musket for collecting any game I might shoot, wooden frames with sheets of paper for pressing plants, and a bag for anything else of interest we might find. Soon we had twenty boxes filled with hundreds of specimens, many of them species never before described by science.

While some of the flora resembled varieties with which I was familiar, many were completely new. Their magnificence stunned me. We indulged in the most thrilling plant hunting either of us had ever experienced. Unfamiliar trees proliferated - purple glory trees, with glossy dark green leaves and deep violet flowers, cecropia trees whose stilt-like-roots made them look as if they could get up and walk away, tabebuia trees sporting their yellow trumpet flowers. Countless stunning orchids, and mysterious bromeliads gleaned sustenance from the air itself with their strangely sinuous air roots.

Despite the pain of his wound, Philibert took the trip to shore every day, hobbling up and down the beach, calling out instructions while I scrambled over the rugged terrain.

The sailors were confined to the ship, but they made a game of watching as Philibert hobbled back and forth calling out instructions to me. They began to call me Philibert's beast of burden, loaded down as I was.

One perfectly ordinary day, as I struggled through the dense shrubbery, a particularly magnificent shrub transfixed me. Its thorny branches were completely covered with riotous garlands of flaming red flowers. It was magnificent. I snatched my magnifying glass from the sac and looked closely. Its delicate, papery flowers resembled a type of bean plant we used at home for treating wounds. I wondered if it could do the same for Philibert. I snipped off a thorny branch and trudged back to the beach.

"Philibert look at this!" I held up the branch like a trophy.

He examined it thoughtfully. "It looks rather like a hibiscus; except the flowers are remarkably dense all the way down the branch, and it's so brilliant! I haven't seen anything like this. Look at these petals. I think they are actually bracts, and not true flowers."

Back in our quarters, Philibert examined every aspect of the plant's anatomy in detail. "I think it's a new plant," he said in a hushed, reverential voice. "I will have the honor of naming it." He hesitated, pondering the decision, then his eyes lit up with delight. "I will name it after our captain."

The next day I stood at Philibert's side as he presented the branch to the captain with as much pomp as he could muster in our modest circumstances.

"Look at this magnificent plant I discovered yesterday," he boasted.

"I have named it Bougainvillea spectabilis, the 'remarkable Bougainvillea', in our captain's honor. I will present it to our captain when we meet in Rio de Janeiro.

A great cheer resonated among the onlookers. Everyone was thrilled except me. It was all I could do to smother a groan of indignation. He could barely walk. I discovered the plant, not Philibert. I sighed and resigned myself to the obscurity of a servant.

* * *

As they had every day, crew men watched with curiosity as I clambered over the coastal landscape. Despite the grudging respect my strength, agility, and devoted service to Philibert earned me, there were persistent rumors that I was not a boy. From the outset Francois Vives, the ship's surgeon, spread gossip about my relationship with Philibert. No hair grew on my chin, my voice remained high-pitched, and though I was strong, I didn't have the well-defined muscles of a youth turning into a man. The crewmen were a superstitious lot, and like untold generations before them, they believed a woman on board would bring bad luck. I kept out of their way and avoided speaking lest my high-pitched voice stirred up suspicion.

Vives held a particular grudge against me and whispered his suspicions into the captain's ear, not only because he suspected I was a girl, but because I was a lowly servant who did not deserve special treatment and was breaking the law by my very presence. There were murmurings that I should be put ashore at the next port to join French colonists who were voyaging back to France. Captain Giraudais was aware of the rumblings among the crew but chose to ignore them.

I could do nothing about the gossip and ill-will swirling around me except remain constantly vigilant and exhibit irreproachable behavior. In the end, reason and practicality won out. It was clear that Philibert's wound, which had never healed or even scabbed over, needed constant medical attention. If it was allowed to fester there was a good possibility gangrene would develop, and he might lose the leg altogether. The captain realized how important my care of Philibert was. Who else would cater to the needs of a botanist appointed by the King himself? After observing our botanical outings, Giraudais came to appreciate that I had the skill and knowledge to help Philibert botanize, and the competence to tend to his health. Reluctantly, he turned a blind eye and allowed me to remain on the ship. I became a ghost.

At the end of April, after only twenty days, our respite in Montevideo ended when two Spanish frigates arrived. Two officers in elegant uniforms disembarked with a message for Captain Gaurdais. He broke the seal and unfolded the paper.

You are hereby ordered to sail to Rio de Janeiro and await Captain Bougainville' s inspection.

Since Bougainville had already been sailing toward the Malouines when *L'Etoile* launched from Rochefort, this would be the first time the two ships would anchor together. Officers and crew of *L'Etoile* muttered nervously anticipating the reckoning that would come when Bougainville inspected the sparsely provisioned hold. The only mission *L'Etoile* had truly accomplished during its days in Montevideo, was to rid itself of the illicit contraband.

Reprovisioning was time-consuming drudgery that went slowly. *L'Etoile's* role was to supply both ships during the voyage. Anyone who looked at the hold would see that essential stocks of food and water were too meager to last for more than a couple of months. Giraudais had failed in his primary mission.

At the end of May *L'Etoile* cast off for Rio de Janeiro to await our rendezvous with Captain Bougainville's ship, the *Boudeuse*. By mid-June we lay at anchor in Rio de Janeiro.

The day of the inspection was breezy and spitting drizzle. Nonetheless, the officers donned their dress uniforms, and with tricorn hats tucked under an arm, they stood at attention on deck as Captain Giraudais with all due ceremony, welcomed Captain

Bougainville on board. Bougainville said nothing as he inspected the officers, but his stern visage, furrowed brows, clenched jaw made his mood perfectly clear.

"We can dispense with the niceties," he said impatiently. "Take me to the hold at once."

They descended the companionway to the cargo hold. From the deck I could hear the voices of Giraudais and Bougainville grow louder. After what seemed like a long time, they re-emerged from the inspection. A red-faced Giraudais was pleading with Bougainville for understanding.

"But you see, sir, we were detained by the inept authorities in Rochefort. They dragged their feet for so long we ran out of time to properly stock the ship. And during the crossing we encountered heavy seas and hurricane force winds. The ship sustained considerable damage and much of our food became waterlogged."

"Be that as it may, your excuses will not fill the bellies of our men for the rest of the voyage. No excuse is a good excuse."

"I will see to it that the *L'Etoile* has provisions for at least ten months, and I will do it quickly," Giraudais pledged. "The welfare of my crew is my utmost concern. I promise I will take care of it." Up to this point, the welfare of the crew consisted primarily of lining their pockets, not stocking the ship.

I couldn't see Bougainville's expression, but I could feel a current of contentiousness as they disappeared into the captain's cabin. It hadn't gone well. After the official formalities and inspections were completed, the officers, scientists, and dignitaries enjoyed a lavish dinner. Philibert returned with a reprise of the dinner conversation and a portion of leftovers for me.

"I was impressed with Captain Bougainville. He has the rigid gravitas of a navy captain, but he is also a scholar. Did you know he published a treatise on calculus when he was twenty-four?"

It was a rhetorical question, of course, so I simply nodded. "Go on," I said.

"He has an impressive military background and a reputation for being a serious, though not cheerless, man. He acquitted himself brilliantly as a military officer in war time. He is determined to plant a French colony on Terre Australis, the great, unknown southern continent in the South Pacific. I don't think I have ever met a more impressive captain. We are in good hands."

Though Philibert was impressionable and prone to excitability, I understood that the other officers, gentlemen, and crew held the captain in highest esteem. It was reassuring that they had such trust in him.

Rio de Janeiro gave us another opportunity to immerse ourselves in nature. The beauty and novelty of Rio de Janeiro called us as a siren's song, making it even more painful when Captain Giraudais decided to sequester Philibert in his quarters for several weeks.

In my opinion, we had Vives to thank for his confinement. Vindictive and jealous as he was, he chose this moment of greatest botanical opportunity to whisper into the captain's ear that Philibert was in imminent danger of developing gangrene.

I had been treating Philibert's injury daily with poultices of comfrey, yarrow, and wine as an antiseptic, packed into a clay plaster bound tightly to his leg. Slowly his wound began to scab over, not perfectly, but well enough that we had hope for a good recovery.

I was livid about being confined. "I cannot believe that Giraudais is clipping your wings now that we have this golden opportunity for discovery. Vives won't be satisfied until he has completely disgraced us."

Philibert was disappointed but accepted the setback with more equanimity than I did. "You misunderstand the captain, Jeanne. He is truly concerned about my condition. He is doing this for my own good. He knows I would never slow down enough to allow my leg to heal. He is protecting me from myself."

I growled under my breath but didn't argue. I could hardly contain my anger because I knew it was Vives, the troublemaker, spreading rumors about my sex and now sidetracking our research. But, if Philibert chose to remain sanguine, then I too would swallow my rage.

On July fifteenth we set sail back to Montevideo. For me at least, some good came of our confinement on board. On nights when the weather was fair, and *L'Etoile* rocked gently on the ripples, I was able to slip undetected to my favorite spot on deck, tucked in among coils of rope, bales and boxes. One of these nights, I found Monsieur

Veron, the ship's astronomer, gazing intently at the heavens through his brass telescope.

"Do you mind if I sit next to you?" My curiosity outweighed my reticence. He looked at me, his expression curious but not judgmental. He did not scold me or shoo me away.

"Are you the botanist's assistant?" He asked politely, then returned his eye back to his telescope.

"Yes, sir, I am, and also his nurse, and valet."

"I see. You are a youth of many talents then." Without a word, he handed me his telescope. "Here, take a look."

In no time, I had lost myself among the uncountable stars in the black sky. I could feel his stare on my smooth face, innocent of any nascent facial hair. And though it made me wary and uncomfortable, I did not take my eye away from the lens.

"Have you ever seen stars this magnificent?" he asked.

"No sir, I've never looked through a telescope. There are stars, behind stars out to infinity."

He smiled. His lush brown hair curled haphazardly around his square face. He was young, not much older than me, but with the self-assurance of a well-heeled, well-educated man. His placid demeanor calmed me, and I felt safe with him. After our first encounter, I felt compelled to join him on deck as often as I could. I was lonely with no one other than Philibert to talk to, and he was as close as I came to companionship. I started to look forward to seeing him.

"So, you are Monsieur Commerson's assistant," he said. It wasn't really a question; he knew the answer. He drew back for a better look at me. I wanted to melt into the tar on the deck, worried he would see beyond my disguise. "That explains your curiosity. I see you investigating the plants wherever we stop. Most deckhands take their view of the night sky for granted, and the other servants have little inquisitiveness." He gently pried the telescope out of my hands and returned to peering through the miraculous tube. "So, your curiosity is a welcome novelty."

I took to meeting him on deck whenever all was quiet and the night watchmen were huddled at the rail gossiping and laughing. Through the lens, the celestial bodies exploded in size. He patiently pointed out the constellations.

He pointed the telescope toward the south. "That is the Southern Cross."

I nodded, not taking my eyes from the sky.

"In the northern realms, the North Star doesn't circle around the sky as the others do. It stays in one place and the other stars and planets circle around it. The Southern Cross serves much the same purpose, circling around the south pole in a tight circle while the others whirl around in their endless meanderings." He watched my face, my chin lifted, mouth slightly open, straining to decipher the Southern Cross.

"Travelers use it to plot their direction. Over there," he guided my gaze to the west. "That is Canis Major, the big dog. Do you see the legs, and the little tail sticking out behind?"

I chuckled when I recognized the tail, as charmed as a girl with a new doll.

"Have you ever seen the constellation, Leo?"

"Yes, I have!" I crowed with pride. I immediately started searching for the familiar form. "There it is! Up there, in the north." Without seeing his face, I could tell he was smiling.

"And that small reddish orb is Mars," my voice rose with excitement.

"You're absolutely right." His respectful attentiveness comforted me like an oasis in an arid, hostile land. He was my respite from tedium and anxiety.

July twenty-fifth was a day I will cherish for the rest of my life. Veron had an important mission on the voyage. He was attempting to devise a method for calculating longitude while at sea. He kept his equipment meticulously clean and adjusted, always ready for perfect viewing. I often watched him as he labored, head down, muttering quietly to himself as he pored over complex calculations and astronomical predictions. That day he gathered anyone who was interested on deck to witness one of the grandest sights in the heavens. Clouds scudded across the sky preventing us from getting a perfect view, but little by little, the dark disc of the moon moved across the face of the sun. Slowly, the moon's shadow consumed the sun until only a sliver, like the crescent of the waning moon, was all that remained visible. The sky became dusky, and even the most hardened seamen grew quiet. A brilliant ring of fire showed vivid red orange from behind the disc of the moon. Veron, with his optical instruments and pages of mathematical calculations had predicted the exact timing of a solar eclipse. His findings proved his forecast perfectly. "Hurrahs!" came from all directions. The young astronomer/mathematician had accurately predicted the eclipse while on water. He smiled like a child at Christmas. I was thrilled for him.

CHAPTER ELEVEN

BUENOS AIRES TO MONTEVIDEO
JULY TO NOVEMBER 1767

By mid-July Captain Bougainville was ready to set sail for the Straits of Magellan, the route, first followed by the Portuguese mariner, Ferdinand Magellan, two hundred and fifty years before. Listening to Philibert's conversations before we left Paris, I learned that, in all that time, only a few expeditions had completed the full circumnavigation. If we accomplished our objective, we would be the first French voyage to do so.

The Portuguese, Spanish, and English captains who managed to find their way through the little-known passage around the southernmost extremity of South America kept their secrets to themselves. The strait was like a dangerous hurdle only the finest racehorse could clear. All Captain Bougainville's talent and experience would be put to the test. The captain ordered both ships, *L'Etoile* and *Boudeuse,* to leave Rio de Janeiro and return to Montevideo to make final preparations and reload provisions and supplies for the next momentous phase of our journey.

We were all in high spirits, busily preparing for our imminent departure. Philibert and I arranged our equipment, planned where the many new specimens we expected to discover could be stored, and hypothesized about the types of plants we might see. All was moving along smoothly when disaster struck.

The night before we were supposed to weigh anchor and sail out of the harbor, a mighty storm suddenly rose up. The ship rocked so violently that we had to grab hold of anything stationary to avoid being thrown overboard like a child's toy. The crewmen tied down the barrels that rolled across the deck threatening to flatten anyone who got in the way. Men scrambled up the rigging to secure the sails to the yardarms swaying perilously in the wind. Just when we thought the storm was abating, the worst of it descended upon us like the jagged teeth of a dragon. A mighty crash shuddered through the entire ship. The officers on deck bellowed orders from all directions. "Lash yourself to the wheel, mate!" "Get the sails off her." "Secure the halyards for heavy weather." "We've lost the bowsprit." "We are shipping water into the hold."

Philibert and I huddled in our cabin, wide-eyed and terrified. No one ordered us to abandon ship, so we clung to the beams, and listened to the howling winds and the sailors shouting. At least no water sloshed into our cabin. Our specimens were jostled and tossed about but not destroyed.

When the winds subsided, I ventured to the topside to view the damage. Veron was already on deck talking to the officers. I sidled up behind him and stood as unobtrusively as possible, until he turned toward me. He didn't acknowledge my presence, and acted as if I was invisible, the perfect response. He did not pay attention to me so neither did anyone else. My wide eyes and raised eyebrows betrayed my alarm, though I said nothing. The less I talked the better. I listened as the first mate explained the havoc the storm had wrought.

"Last night the harbor was crowded," he explained. I nodded, remembering the skillful maneuvers the ship had to take to find anchorage among the many ships sheltered in the harbor when we arrived. "During the turbulence of the storm, the anchor of one of the ships tore free and dragged across the bottom, ripping out the anchors of several nearby ships. It was chaos. One of the unmoored ships ploughed into *L'Etoile,* tearing off the bowsprit and gouging a sizeable hole in the prow. The damage is serious. It is going to take quite some time to repair. Captain Bougainville and Captain Giraudais will assess the destruction. The officers tell us, the *Boudeuse* fared a little better, because she has a deeper draft and was farther out into the shipping channel with the larger ships and was not as crowded, so she sustained less damage."

It did not take Captain Bougainville long to determine that the forests around Montevideo were so depleted that they couldn't provide sufficient timber for the extensive repairs *L'Etoile* needed. He didn't have much time to make a decision. *L'Etoile* was shipping water through the breach punched in its side and the gaping hole where the bowsprit used to be. He ordered both ships to sail west, toward a remote estuary near Buenos Aires where the mouth of Rio de la Plata River empties into the bay. Both ships desperately needed restoration before they could face the rigors of the Straits of Magellan, and beyond that, the immense Pacific Ocean.

When *L"Etoile* and the *Boudeuse* limped into the sanctuary at high tide, the captain found a steep beach and ordered the ships to be brought up broadside to the shore. When the tide receded, the ships were left high and dry on the beach. All the crewman scurried to strip down the ships. They removed every movable item. My job was hauling our specimen cases, plant presses, and smaller equipment to shore.

As quick as the lash of a whip, the experienced sailors shot orders at the new men. The upper parts of the masts, all the rigging, and shredded sails were hauled to the beach. Next, the cannons, powder, and ammunition came off the ships so the men could seal the gun ports. They toiled for several days until the great ships lay naked on the sand. I couldn't prevent harrowing thoughts from plaguing me. What if another storm destroyed our naked ships as they laid there on the beach as vulnerable as a baby on a bucking horse.

Exhausted as they were, they were not yet finished. First, they attached thick ropes to the mastheads. To the boatswain's rhythmic chant, "heave ho, heave ho," the men hauled in unison on thick ropes until the ships healed over on their sides exposing the hulls to the light of day. Like ants on jelly, the crewmen swarmed over them, repairing torn rigging, stitching shredded sails, caulking leaks, scraping barnacles and algae from the keel. They scrubbed mold from damp wood and replaced rotted boards.

With the ship rolled over on its side, its keel facing skyward, *L'Etoile* revealed a secret she had been hiding. An entire section of the hull had never been caulked, and there were two augur holes that had not been plugged. We had been sailing on a ship as leaky as a sieve. It was clear we would be at our anchorage south of Buenos Aires for quite some time. It took weeks of hard work to make the ships seaworthy again.

For Philibert and me this was a wonderful opportunity to explore the glorious forests behind the beach. This remote area near Buenos Aires proved to be even richer in plant life than Montevideo. We left it to the ship's crew to rebuild and re-outfit *L'Etoile,* while we once again prowled the tropical forests. The herb woman in me rejoiced when I found fennel and calla lilies, plants as familiar they as my backyard in La Comelle. But that was rare. Most of the vegetation was completely alien.

Philibert's injured leg had improved considerably after his enforced confinement, and he was in high spirits. He turned his eye to analyzing the new specimens we collected. "We are going to have the devil of a time preserving these cacti," he complained, gingerly holding a prickly pear pad in his tongs. "They are well armed against browsers. These long spines are dangerous enough, but each one nestles in a little bed of tiny needles that burrow into the skin if touched. You don't want to touch those," he explained. "You can pull a spine out of your skin, but these little needles can burrow in and never come out. The pads store water, and if we press them in our field presses, they will ooze a cloudy liquid. Come look closely at these pads. What do you see?"

I bent over his shoulder as he picked off tiny, sticky, white pillows scattered over the cactus pads. "Now, look at this." He carefully scraped the substance off the pad and squeezed it between his thumb nails. A red ooze trickled down his fingers.

"It almost looks like it's bleeding," I poked gingerly at the sticky white film.

"You're not far off," he grinned. "If I'm right, we have found a secret the Spanish have been guarding for two centuries. I have read about this but have never seen it. The red substance is created by a tiny insect called cochineal. The white mass is its cocoon. It's used to make a vibrant red dye. This is exactly the type of discovery that will please the King. If we can raise these plants successfully in France, we will be able to destroy Spain's monopoly. It would revolutionize France's fabric industry."

I scooped up a little ball of white goo and squeezed it between my thumb nails as Philibert had done. Bright red drops oozed out. I was elated. This was far more exciting than finding the familiar fennel or lily.

During our four-month stay outside of Buenos Aires a much-improved Philibert and I tramped across the landscape, making new botanical discoveries every day.

"It is like having the Garden of Eden entirely to ourselves," Philibert enthused. We had plenty to explore. Grasslands, marshes, and wet woodlands nourished an enormous variety of life. By the time we left the bay near Buenos Aires I had carefully curated several hundred of the species we had collected, labeling them with the time and date we had collected them. Philibert assigned them proper Latin names, using the clever system his friend Carl Linnaeus recently invented. Our curiosity wasn't confined to plants. Philibert drew sketches and made careful notes about shells, stony and soft corals, birds, lizards, and a new species of river dolphin. The birds were especially spectacular, kiting through the forests displaying a wanton diversity of vibrant colors.

We were only a few kilometers outside of town, but the handprint of man was barely visible in this pristine wilderness. Buenos Aires itself was a small, ramshackle town with rough huts that could hardly be called houses. Within a few short years our garden of Eden would be a distant memory, displaced and disfigured by another repulsive city. By the time the ships were worthy of the challenge before us, four months had passed.

CHAPTER TWELVE

STRAITS OF MAGELLAN &
PATAGONIA
DECEMBER 1767 TO JANUARY 1768

By November, the ships were repaired and the time to continue our voyage had finally arrived. Cattle tromped up the gangway to pens in the hold. Chickens squawked and shrieked in their cages as if the ax was already hovering over their necks. Barrels of flour nestled alongside barrels of fresh water, dried meat, and a considerable number of brandy casks. I was delighted to see masses of vegetables deposited next to the dry biscuit and salted meat that made up our usual diet at sea.

On November fourteenth, almost a year after we left France, we set sail once again. Our relief to be under sail once more did not last long. No sooner had we made the mouth of the Rio de la Plata Bay, than we encountered heavy weather, gale-force winds, and contrary currents. They seemed to come from every direction at once rocking us about as if *L'Etoile* was no more substantial than a baby's crib. The yardarm that held our topsail split with a deafening wail and dangled from the mast, with its sail flapping like laundry hung out to dry, and despite the repairs we had just made, *L'Etoile* was taking on water again. Worst of all, only two of our cherished cattle survived the storm's violent thrashing. The voyage was months behind schedule and Captain Bougainville was in no mood for further delay, so as soon as the weather calmed we sailed on.

Once out of the harbor, we charted a course southward toward the Strait of Magellan. The great oceanic desert of the mid-Atlantic was now behind us. The coastal waters were warm and teemed with life. Huge birds with eight-foot wingspans glided effortlessly above us. The old tars told us they almost never alighted on the land, preferring to sail the skies for incredibly long distances.

Philibert and I put our time to good use, sorting through the hundreds of plants crowding our cabin. It was an endless task, but we labored away, naming, labeling and classifying our growing collection.

We followed the shore but stayed far enough away from land to avoid being driven aground by high winds. Delightful new creatures appeared daily. Whenever I could, I escaped from our cabin with its swampy smells to stand at the rail hoping to spot the curious sea creatures following the ship. Porpoises sliced through the sea, leaping above the surface then disappearing again beneath the waves. The sea lions charmed me. They popped their dog-like heads above water to look at us with large, intelligent black eyes, as curious about us as we were about them. Stiff whiskers protruded from their cheeks and little ears laid back against their heads. They had flippers for arms and two misshapen appendages at their tail end where their feet should have been. It was an effort to resist the temptation to hop up and down like a gleeful child. I struggled to maintain my composure watching them slice through the water like arrows shot from a bow.

Flocks of odd little penguins, with black backs, white bellies, and feathers so slick and glossy they appeared to be painted on, congregated along the rocky shores. I would not have believed they were birds until Philibert convinced me.

"Yes, they are birds," he insisted when I questioned him, "but they cannot fly. See how they waddle clumsily, flapping their short, stiff, wings when walking on land? Those wings are totally useless for flight, but once they launch themselves into the sea, they knife through the water at breathtaking speeds, darting, rolling and twisting in pursuit of the fish they preyed upon. You'll see."

We watched them waddle gracelessly along the shore. Their long, tubular shape made them look like fat sausages with fins and flippers. If Philibert hadn't told me, I would never have guessed they were birds. Once they dove into the water, however, they were lightning fast, just as Philibert had said. Their speed and agility reminded me of the acrobatics of swallows, darting low over the ponds then soaring high, turning and twisting as they chased their prey.

Porpoises followed us, cavorting next to the ship. Like the black and white penguins, their chubby bodies looked like they were painted by an artist who loved sharp contrasts, with heads, dorsal fins, and flukes as black and glossy as pitch contrasting with gleaming white bellies. Dozens of them traveled in packs diving under the water, reappearing suddenly, racing alongside the ship, leaping out of the water, playfully surfing our wake, then disappearing beneath the waves.

Most dramatic of all were the whales. Before we sailed, I might have had to stretch my imagination to visualize sea lions, penguins, and dolphins, but nothing could have prepared me for the sight of the whales.

One morning as Philibert and I slaved away, boisterous cries from the deck wrenched us away from our work. Not knowing if we were about to run aground, ram another ship, or spring a fatal leak, we scurried up the gangway to the deck.

The barrelman in the crow's nest pointed at four enormous creatures moving toward us. Each one was half as long as the ship. The lead animal rolled on its side exposing its white belly. One long flipper waved above the water then smacked down with a tremendous splash. The beast righted itself, swimming on its belly like a fish, and suddenly a spray of water exploded into the air from a fissure on the top of its monstrous head. The cleft closed and the whale arced gracefully downward. All that remained in sight was a massive tail fin, dripping with water waving in the air. Before its entire body disappeared into the deep, the beast flipped its tail straight up then slapped the surface with a tremendous 'thwack'. My heart beat so hard I could feel my pulse in my ears. A second whale launched vertically out of the water, rolled on its side and crashed down, creating a great wave so large it rocked the ship. Its white underside was strewn about with irregular black flecks, and its enormous white neck was incised with parallel striations. One after another, the four whales leapt, twisted, and crashed into the water. Some heaved themselves so far out of the water they seemed to pirouette on their tail flukes in a dramatic display of what could only be pure joy. What else could motivate these leviathans to exhibit such unbridled exuberance? They weren't fishing or eating but performing a gargantuan water ballet. It was thrilling beyond words.

* * *

On December second Captain Bougainville, with the help of Monsieur Veron's telescope, spotted the Cape of Virgins at the entrance to the Strait of Magellan. This would be the most dangerous leg of our voyage. The Portuguese, Spanish and British had already conquered this tortuous passage to the Pacific, often at the cost of hundreds of lives. If we succeeded, we would be the first French ship to do so.

The great maritime powers were rivals who did not share information about routes, shoals, tides or currents in the treacherous channel. A somber mood spread over the crew, disquieted by a combination of anticipation and anxiety. Though they had supreme faith in their Captain who was known for his extensive experience and even temperament, even so, he had never faced the hazards of this passage.

I stood at the rail, with hands clasped behind my back, as emotionless as a sphinx, as our great ships majestically rounded the corner into the capacious Possession Bay marking our entry into the strait.

For one day we rested, like a runner gathering his strength before a race. The entry to the bay was wide, but by the next day it narrowed like a baker's funnel. The gap between Patagonia to our north and Tierra del Fuego to our south shrank down to a perilously narrow passage, made more dangerous by the rocks that jutted into the gap. Rocky palisades replaced gravelly beaches. Cliffs thrust up on both sides like fortress walls. Sometimes they were miles apart and sometimes breathtakingly close. A bewildering tide, confounding currents and contrary winds opposed us. A chaos of disorganized crashing waves broke over us.

The captain's cry - "Take the sounding!" - passed from one deck hand to another. Soon a strapping seaman hauling a heavy lead weight and coils of rope draped over his shoulder scrambled up the rigging to stand on a cross beam. He swung the weight back and forth, gaining momentum with each sweep, then let it loose. As the weight splashed into the water, he played out the rope out until it landed on the bottom, and he called out the water's depth. "Thirty-five fathoms." Moments later he sang out again. "Twenty fathoms." I had no idea how deep the water needed to be to accommodate *L'Etoile* and the much larger *Boudeuse* but Philibert did, and his brow furrowed, as he stood very still gripping the rail, hardly breathing. When the depth of five fathoms was called out near panic overtook the crew. No one wanted to face the dire consequences of running aground in shallow water amid towering rocky pillars. The captain barked out orders until he positioned the vessels close to the rocky palisades where the water was deeper. We dropped anchor and Philibert's breathing returned to normal.

For two days, battling hard winds and strong, opposing currents, the captain tried repeatedly to thread the needle of the narrow passage, but each time he was forced to retreat. The paralyzing fear that accompanies uncertainty strangled me. On the third day the weather calmed, and we effortlessly threaded the needle between the two cliffs and emerged into a small bay. There, arrayed on the shore, stood several robust men and their horses waving a white flag as they watched us. How peculiar it was for these primitive men to possess a perfectly rectangular, carefully stitched white cloth.

"I have never seen native people before, but doesn't that seem odd to you?" I asked   Philibert.

"It was no doubt given to them by a previous expedition," Philibert speculated. "Others have navigated the strait before us."

The captain answered by hoisting our ships' flags. I marveled at these beautiful men. They were well-muscled, with long black hair. There they stood, nearly naked, with heavy cloaks covering their shoulders and only a leather patch covering their private parts.

"They must be very resistant to the cold," I commented. "Even though it is the middle of summer here, it is still cold enough to freeze shallow water."

"I'm sure they are," Philibert answered. "Imagine what hardships the rigors of winter must bring."

The captain launched one longboat from each ship, carrying officers and scientists. Philibert and I were among them. A few Marines came with us as bodyguards.

I held my body rigid, my back straight, and stared fixedly ahead. This was our first encounter with native tribesmen, and I knew from the sailors' conversations, that Europeans sometimes did not survive such encounters. I was honored to be chosen for first contact but terrified.

I understood from Philibert that the most common interaction when first meeting native people was to exchange gifts, a universal signal of good intentions. So that's what the captain did. We stood in an orderly line along the beach facing the Americans. I was wonder struck as the natives dismounted from their horses and walked toward us with arms outstretched in friendly greeting. Our men handed out bread and cakes from our larder. The men devoured the food in moments. In exchange they gave us guanaco skins. We had seen these placid grazing animals on the hillsides as we passed by. They looked like small camels with long slender necks, fine-boned legs and luxurious silky fur. Remarkably, the men did not fear us, nor did they seem surprised to see us. They appeared to be familiar with our muskets and imitated the sharp, booming sounds they made when fired. They mimed the motions of smoking and made signs indicating they wanted tobacco. Clearly, they had encountered other Europeans and were quite familiar with our possessions.

Philibert and I immediately set about gathering plants. These remarkably friendly people watched us intently, curious about everything I did. I imagined they wondered why we were acting so foolishly, but they helped us nonetheless, scouring the area, bringing plants they plucked from the dry soil. The Patagonians watched me with great interest and soon began bringing plants to me. Their kindness warmed me.

As the amber sun sank toward the horizon, we packed up our new floral finds, boarded the longboats and rowed back to the ships. The Patagonians walked alongside our departing boats, wading into the icy water to see us off.

For five days we returned to shore to gather plants. We resumed the same method we used in Montevideo, with Philibert standing on the pebbly beach while I scaled rock faces, and slid down scree slopes, thoroughly exploring the vicinity in freezing temperatures scraping my shins, hands and feet raw.

The first plant I harvested was familiar, Patagonia's version of Bilberry. It would be useful for treating the disease common among crewmen who fraternized with loose women in port towns. Heaven only knew how many of them would need treatment. The alternative, the mercury Vives usually dispensed, produced such ugly physical and mental side-effects it was almost worse than the disease.

I gathered as many plants as I could, as fast as I could. Almost everything I collected was new to me. I could not take the time for close study until we were back at sea when I would have plenty of hours to fill. The exhilaration of discovery outweighed the physical challenge of scrambling over the rugged landscape. In fact, I welcomed the strenuous effort.

The one thing that dampened my enjoyment was being watched. The crewmen who did not have a specific task on shore were not allowed to disembark. Many of the idle seamen stood on deck and watched every move I made. I hoped that my vigorous activity would deflect their suspicions about my sex. As hard as I worked, there was always subterfuge swirling around me. Vives delighted in denigrating my activities and fomenting doubt about my sex. By this time, Captain Bougainville, the officers and fellow scientists aboard, barely noticed me and treated me as they would any other servant. But Vives' whispered accusations rippled through the ranks of crewmen.

By the end of the fifth day in Patagonia, I was nearing exhaustion and had lost patience with the voyeurism of the sailors. My feet and legs were scored by lesions, blisters, and bruises. My bound chest never gave me a moment's comfort, so I finally spoke up to Philibert. "Can't you do something to discourage the men on deck from scrutinizing my every move?"

"What are you talking about? Why should that trouble you? We are doing what we came here to do. Focus on that. Forget about the men. Why would you care anyway? No one is questioning your sex."

"Don't you remember the terrifying night I spent in the men's quarters when I had to point a loaded pistol at their heads to keep them at bay?"

"Oh heavens! That's all in the past. No one thinks of that anymore."

"You think not?" I challenged him. "That weasel, Vives, never misses an opportunity to deride me and spread suspicion among the men. He would see me thrown overboard if he had a chance."

"Stop worrying. Just take your rifle, your plant press, and the rest of your equipment and do your job. I'm not worrying about them, and neither should you."

If I had any illusions about Philibert protecting me in any way, I was totally free of that notion. I knew he would not help me, would do nothing to stop the rumors, and would turn a blind eye to my concerns. My respect for my one-time lover, father of my abandoned child, totally evaporated like a shallow puddle under a blazing sun. We were still working partners, cabin-mates, colleagues, and I was still his nurse. But our affection had died.

By the end of our time on the Patagonian beach, I had bagged shells, lichen covered rocks, mossy mats, ferns, and flowers. My hands were red and sore, my legs scraped and bruised. Still, it was very satisfying. I ended each day with a sense of accomplishment, even though I knew Philibert would receive all the praise. I couldn't let that bother me. A servant is only a servant. I had very little education, no money or property. That would never change. I reminded myself that I would not be here at all were it not for him. I wouldn't let jealousy, anger, and disillusionment spoil this life-changing experience.

On December eleventh, the captain determined that conditions were right to resume our journey, and we left our anchorage. With a cooperative tide and favorable winds billowing the sails, we headed toward the second neck in the strait. It was not as narrow as the first, but more dangerous rocks loomed around us threatening to lacerate the ships' hulls. Agreeable weather never lasted for long in these latitudes, and soon violent squalls, and pounding rains scoured the decks. Philibert and I had no sooner retired to our cabin than we heard hail bouncing off the deck above us. The ship slowed, stopped, dropped anchor again, and we rode out the storm. The following day, the squall abated, the ships avoided serious damage, so we headed to Elizabeth Island.

Elizabeth Island could not have been more different from our previous stop if it had been on another planet. The soil here was dry and dusty and nurtured very little life. A tiny, delicate, blue-eyed grass with violet flowers was almost the only plant that grew here, creating a dense gray-green mat close to the ground to escape from the lacerating winds. *Sisyrinchium chilense.*

The captain ordered Philibert, and I with several crewmen to shore to document what we found there, but another blast of icy wind and rain left us with without shelter. The first mate ordered me and several of the men to dig up mats of turf with which to construct a wind break. I was a servant boy, and the men had seen how strong I was, so I could hardly object. I spent a damp, miserable, freezing night on the island, my back aching from digging turf for the entire landing party.

The following day was no better. Finally, on December thirteenth we began again. This time we encountered swirling eddies and relentless winds. Even the captain declared that the weather here must be the worst in all the world. The men in the rigging adjusted, readjusted, furled and unfurled sails in a fruitless effort to keep the ships moving forward. The winds waged combat with the ships. The wind won. It overpowered the ships, forcing us into a great inlet on the shore of Tierra del Fuego. The captain found an anchorage with a sandy bottom where we finally slept without a storm raging. Paradoxically, the wind weakened so much that for two days there was too little wind to fill the sails.

The view was stunning and varied, with wide stone beaches, steep hills, and rivers plummeting down from wooded uplands. Knowing we were at the southernmost reaches of the planet gave me a special perspective. Rather than dominating nature, we were as vulnerable to its the whims as a house of cards, and far less well adapted than the tiny flowers or twisted trees.

The mornings at the bottom of the world were gloomy. Though it was the height of the Antarctic summer, we could hardly tell day from night. The sun never truly set in this place. It skirted the western horizon, dipped below it for a couple of hours, and came up again in the east. It was never fully dark nor fully light. Time stood still. When the longboats deposited us on shore to search for herbs, we faced gloomy skies, freezing drizzle, and numbing temperatures.

Miserable as the weather was, it was a unique opportunity to forage for plants in this isolated place. How many other botanists had visited these latitudes? We were among a select few. Unlike the lush tropical varieties we harvested in Montevideo, this bay sheltered weather-hardened species adapted to the extreme conditions. An abundance of tiny flowers huddled close to the ground blooming in the Antarctic summer. The only evergreens that grew were contorted into hideous shapes. The nearly constant wind kept them hugging the ground so tightly they reached only a few feet high. The branches facing the wind had no needles and bent away from the wind as if clawing their way toward escape. Yet these bizarrely deformed trees survived. Other plants were similarly hardy and resilient species sheltered beneath the limbs of the tortured trees, hidden away from the fierce winds that seemed never to abate. What seemed another unwanted detour to the captain was a singular opportunity for us.

When we left the anchorage, the strait turned a new face toward us. Enormous walls of ice, so tall they reached into the low clouds, closed in on all sides. Awe washed over me when I peered into the water. The depth of the ice below the surface equaled the height of the ice that towered above. The submerged ice was a brilliant, translucent blue as clear as glass. I was so moved by the miraculous spectacle I had to wipe away tears, so they didn't freeze to my face.

On December sixteenth the weather cleared. The captain took advantage of the weather to sail through the night to a sheltered cove on Cape Forward. Here, on December seventeenth, we established a more permanent camp where we stayed until the end of December. The ships had been battered by storms, soaked by ceaseless torrents, the rigging shredded by winds until they groaned as if tormented. Logs already neatly cut and stacked awaited us, perhaps left behind by previous voyagers.

The Patagonians again came to the beach to greet us, this time with fox pelts to trade. They approached us openly with no fear. We made our trade with the Patagonians, practical knives and decorative beads in exchange for luxurious fox furs. They were accustomed to European dress, but nothing had prepared them for the sight of Prince of Nassau-Siegen. The prince decided to greet the Patagonians with a regal display. All eyes focused on the prince. He was indeed a sight to see. Skin-tight silk stockings and velvet, knee-length breeches clung to his legs. His thigh-length velvet jacket flared out from waist to knees. Elaborate embroidery embellished his jacket, and his linen shirt, all of it was topped off with decorated cuffs and cravat. The Patagonians assumed he was a woman, while they assumed I, standing next to him in my worn-out sailor's garb, was a boy. What an ironic contrast we made. Philibert laughed loudly and I could hardly suppress a chuckle.

Their mutual love of botany drew Philibert and the prince toward each other. They became friends who genuinely enjoyed the other's company, and when the prince asked to join our botanizing expeditions, Philibert was more than happy to include him. The two of them made a comical sight, making their way across the pebbly beaches, Nassau-Siegen-Siegen teetering on his high heeled shoes, and Philibert hobbling on his wounded leg. I trudged along behind them, hauling plant press, leather field satchel, collecting nets and our day's provisions.

Further down the shore, a colony of hundreds of the most grotesque behemoths imaginable stopped us in our tracks. They were built like seals but were huge. The big males were as long as three men laid out end-to-end. Their pendulous noses flopped down over their mouths. The moment rival males approached each other, they rose high on their front flippers and emitted a guttural, grumbling roar. I couldn't decide if they were hilarious or hideous as they rushed at each other slamming their chests together. The females were tiny by comparison, about one-third the size of the males. Unperturbed, they basked in the sun, flipping sand over their backs, mostly ignoring the males and trying to stay out of their way. The pups, with their brown fur and large black eyes, were as appealing as the males were repulsive.

"I've seen these animals. They are called elephant seals," the prince said. "Let's get closer." And he fearlessly strode off among the jumble of blubbery bodies. Philibert grinned and limped along after the handsome young aristocrat.

Their camaraderie grew daily. I could hardly resent Philibert for making friends with a man with whom he could share his love of nature, but it made me irrelevant. I was just a boy, a servant, no longer a partner. That realization, however, did not diminish the awe and wonder I felt walking among these beasts. They showed us no aggression. In fact, they took almost no notice of us at all. It was a slightly woozy, other-worldly experience, as if I was walking through the dreamscape of an extremely intoxicated person.

We did not abandon our mission to collect as many herbs as we could find. I had all but lost track of the total number of specimens we had harvested thus far, but I knew that the tally of plants never-before analyzed exploded with each new day.

For more than two weeks, we acclimatized ourselves to the polar weather as best we could and took advantage of having twenty hours of daylight. But returning to camp at the end of the day reminded us of the problems that remained.

With much of the heaviest cargo offloaded on to the beach, the hulls of our battered ships lay exposed. *L'Etoile's* leak had reopened, and the *Boudeuse* was encrusted with barnacles. Both ships needed repair, but there were very few trees of usable size, and our waterlogged provisions could not be replaced.

Our friend, Monsieur Veron's clever apparatus for measuring longitude would not function normally this close to the southern extreme of the earth, his frustrations dimmed my pleasure. We knew his project was one of the main goals of our voyage. He was disconsolate. Philibert tried to comfort him by pointing out that he had succeeded in measuring longitude at most of the other points of our voyage with a clever instrument of his own invention, but he was still disappointed.

Our bivouac in *Patagonia* turned out to be our longest pause since leaving Montevideo. We knew it was ending when, on December twenty-nineth, the captain sent the longboats out to scout for a possible route to the Pacific. When they returned, the expedition resumed, and we followed the scouts through a maze of channels past towering glacier-hewn rocks, until we emerged from a narrow, dangerous, labyrinth into a limitless expanse of open ocean. The Pacific Ocean opened its wide arms to us. Suddenly the horizon spread out as far as the eye could see. Everyone was overjoyed. Coarse, weather-hardened voices rang out joyfully as we reached the great ocean and the crew sang the Te Deum: "We praise thee, Oh God the Father everlasting. . . Heaven and earth adore thee. . . Holy, holy, holy, Lord God of hosts. Heaven and earth are full of Thy glory."

CHAPTER THIRTEEN

VOYAGE TO TAHITI
JANUARY 22, 1768 TO APRIL 2, 1769

How can I describe the sight of the ocean called Pacific? When we finally watched the western coast of South America sink below the horizon, all certainty about our journey's route sank with it. Philibert and I took advantage of smooth water to gaze at the tranquil sea from a deck that was not pitching and rolling. The sea before us earned its name, the Peaceful Ocean. Starlight reflecting on the ripples resembled fireflies dancing beneath the moon. The days rolled by, as we sailed northwest. The temperature warmed and the persecutions of the Strait of Magellan faded like a bad dream. It had taken us fifty-two fearful, freezing days to pass through the strait. Our perseverance against ice, sleet, furious wind, and corkscrew currents rewarded us with a treasure trove of botanical specimens.

"Now, at last, we will have time to label, describe, and name our collection. But, finding room in the cabin could be a challenge," Philibert said.

"Yes it will, but I can't wait to begin. We can lay our plant cases end to end on top of the crates. That will create a makeshift table where I can arrange them in logical order," I chirped. "Then we'll need to find a safe way to store them. The cabin seemed so spacious when we began our voyage, but now it's impossibly crowded." Philibert nodded in agreement.

Many samples already hung from the rafters to dry. Every day I meticulously inspected every leaf and stem, picking off insects and larvae. I pressed the dried plants between layers of absorbent paper and stored them in the sturdy boxes the ship's carpenter had generously made for us.

I spent most of my time below deck in the safety of our cabin. It became a cherished retreat for me. No more intrusive eyes inspecting my every move. Occasionally, something extraordinary lured me up to the deck. One day Philibert hurried down into the cabin bubbling with excitement. "Come quickly," he tugged at my elbow.

He didn't need to ask twice. The elation in his voice propelled me up the gangway to the deck.

"There!" he bellowed pointing to the water. I surveyed the grey-green water but saw nothing notable. Then I spotted what was making Philibert so excited.

Even after seeing sea lions, elephant seals, penguins, whales and porpoises, this creature was incomparable. There below us, several large, flat, diamond-shaped bodies with elongated wing-like fins, flapped majestically next to the ship. It took several minutes of awestruck gawking to identify the slits on the underside of its "wings" as gills. Protruding from the front of its body, two appendages almost like arms or horns reached outward. Eyes peered out at the base of each of those "arms." Their appearance was so other-worldly, my jaw hung open and my knees almost buckled. When one of them opened its mouth, I took a step back from the rail. A yawning cave, big enough to swallow a man opened. The typical cacophony on deck quieted as all eyes watched these bizarre, majestic creatures. Eventually they turned away from us, an armada of ghostly shadows flapping off as gracefully as birds.

After surviving the extreme cold, I was glad to be warm again, but as we neared the equator my bindings chafed my skin until it was raw and red. I had been regularly applying a poultice of bougainvillea leaves and seed pods to Philibert's leg wound which never seemed to heal. I thought the same poultice might tame my angry rash. During this peaceful part of the voyage, I was in the cabin nearly every day working hard on our collection. In the privacy of our quarters, I removed my cursed bindings and prayed that I would never again need to use them. I should have remembered the lesson from Aesop's Fables "Be careful what you wish for, lest it come true." While I labeled hundreds of specimens, with the date and place where each was collected, Philibert spent most of his time on deck with the crew scanning the horizon for land. The search for land became a communal effort, every available pair of eyes was enlisted in the search.

On March twenty-second, they were successful. Philibert called me up on deck. "Look," he pointed toward the horizon. "See those low islands covered with coconut trees? As enticing as those islands look, they are too small to have a suitable place to stop. We are searching for an island with a bottom solid enough to hold an anchor and large enough to hold pools of fresh water." He looked away from the horizon and directly into my eyes, as serious as the grave. "The captain says we need to find that special island soon. Do you understand?"

I certainly did understand. After all we had lost in transit, I knew we needed to find supplies very soon. Now, everyone focused on finding that hoped-for island. *L'Etoile* skimmed along near the shores of several islands, as close as we dared to go. The larger Boudeuse needed more depth so it sailed in deeper water. The first mate found a larger island where we could get close enough to see more than coconut palms. As we got nearer, we heard muffled, rhythmic drumming. There on the beach, a crowd of naked, dark-skinned men pounded the ground in unison with their thick wooden staffs, occasionally shaking them menacingly in the air and shrieking.

"This would be a lovely place to botanize if only we could get ashore," I said gazing at the idyllic landscape. "Look at all that greenery. Just think of all the new plants that must be growing there. The island is so far from any other land its plants must be unique."

"Look past the shore," Philibert pointed inland. "There, through the trees, is a lovely lagoon. What a heavenly setting this is. But the coral reef that rings the shore protects it like a fortress. And if we somehow manage to reach land, the islanders will make us regret it."

He was right, so we sailed on, past island after tiny island. White curls of water outlined the margins of the coral reefs that defended the beaches. I wondered why the captain didn't deploy the longboats and try to get closer. Maybe they could find a route between the obstacles, but one look at the angry natives, and it became apparent that, even if they could land there, it would be too dangerous.

On April third, a substantially larger island finally appeared. Its aqua-marine waters ringed black sand beaches. As we surveyed the shore looking for suitable anchorage, a flotilla of pirogues surrounded our ships. The bronzed skin of the natives accentuated their virile, healthy appearance. The exchange of goods establishing our mutual good intentions began. The islanders handed bunches of bananas and coconuts up to us as our men tossed small articles of clothing, caps and handkerchiefs, down to them. The natives prized exotic European goods, and in return, they offered us their most delicious fruits. The next day they returned, this time with women. By any measure, these women were the comeliest the men had ever seen. They wore wreaths of beautiful flowers around their necks, and silky black hair cascading down their backs. From the waist up, that was all they wore. After their long abstinence from carnal pleasure, the sailors clamored to go to shore.

Captain Bougainville forbade them to leave the ship, until he established some rules meant to respect the natives and their customs.

That night one young sailor, a cook, defied orders and, under cover of darkness, swam ashore. The next day, I watched as the natives brought him back to the ship. The sailors surrounded him slavering to hear a salacious story of promiscuity. They were disappointed. First, the cook had to explain his experience to the captain. Soon his story spread among the crewmen as fast as fire in dry brush. Philibert shared it with me.

"It was the cook who snuck off," Philibert explained. "We are moored very close to those black sand beaches, and the boy is a good swimmer. He had no trouble swimming the short distance to shore. The natives offered him his choice of beautiful young girls. The boy picked out a smiling, dark-eyed beauty about his own age, grabbed her hand and tried to run off with her into the bushes. But before he could escape, several of the men surrounded him. They removed every scrap of his clothing, and as he stood there, as naked as Adam in the garden, they examined every inch of his body, patting and touching him all over, remarking among themselves about his appearance and his sexual endowments. Never had the boy endured such a humiliating examination." Philibert chuckled, picturing this young man with his hands cupped around his private parts, jerking and twisting to break free from the groping hands. "Then they brought the girl to him and made lewd gestures ordering him to perform the act before them for their entertainment. At that point, the poor boy's masculinity deserted him." Now Philibert was laughing so hard he could barely speak. "By the time he managed to escape and make it back to the ship, he was as rattled as a Spanish maraca."

The ship's men found the story hilarious and teased and taunted the poor young man mercilessly. I couldn't share their glee. I could only imagine what would have happened if it had been me. I did not have to wonder for long. Knowing that the natives were not hostile, Philibert and I began botanizing again. After many long weeks inside our cabin, it was heavenly to work in this paradise. My excitement overwhelmed my fear of confronting the natives. We had hardly begun collecting when several Tahitian men surrounded us. I was crippled by anxiety. Several men closed in on me, cupping their male members in one hand, and pointing at me with the other, calling back and forth to each other. I imagined I was about to undergo the same examination that the cook endured. One man stepped forward repeating the word *"mahu, mahu."*

Before the situation got out of control, the first lieutenant who had accompanied us for our protection, hurried me back to the longboat and rowed me back to *L'Etoile*.

There could be no mistaking the meaning of those gestures. The Tahitian men took one look at me and saw through my disguise. They singled me out for inspection to verify their conclusion that I was a girl. The incident shattered my belief that I could pass as a boy among the natives. I was devastated. The crewmen who had grown accustomed to seeing me as a boy, now became suspicious. Vives' gossip mongering had already cast doubt on my sex and the islanders' reaction to me reinforced their suspicions. Anxiety about what would happen to me now that my secret was discovered overwhelmed me.

Unsurprisingly, I was called before *L'Etoile's* Captain Giraudais. He raised his eyes from the welter of maps laid out before him. When I entered his room, his face fell and he ran a hand through his wavey, greying hair. He looked at me like a parent looks at an errant child. Before he could even speak, I started blubbering.

"I, I, I'm sorry," I stuttered. "Whatever you do with me, please understand Philibert had no part in this. I lied to him when I became his valet. I sincerely believed I could pass as a youth without causing any trouble. I've done this before." The words that tumbled out were a mixture of truth and fiction, the most persuasive fiction I could conjure. "While living in Paris, I served as a valet for a Genevan gentleman. I was an orphan, unprotected and naïve. I was meant to inherit a substantial amount of money with which I could live a humble, but honest life. But I lost my inheritance to the chicanery of an unscrupulous lawyer who stole it from me. I was destitute and hopeless. I judged that dressing as a young man was my best chance of earning a respectable living." I stopped trying to choke back unwelcome tears and let them flow freely.

"Well, your secret is out now. I must say, it's been an open secret for quite some time. But now, the men will feel free to take whatever liberties with you they can steal," Giraudais sighed. "At best they will blame you for any misfortune that might befall us. Everyone knows women on a ship bring bad luck." His eyebrows knitted together, and he glared at me. "At worst . . . Well, let's just say, if I were you, I would make myself as invisible as possible."

For ten days we laid at anchor in Tahiti. I was tarnished by shame. But I was as angry as I was humiliated. Really, what had I done? I had been helpful, hard-working, reliable, strong and as skilled in botany as anyone I knew. I tackled every rugged landscape, and every extreme climate we encountered, while Philibert hobbled along the shore. And now I was disgraced as if I had brought the furies down from the heavens to throw lightning bolts at the ships. Did Philibert come to my defense? No! He stood by as humiliation and contempt were heaped upon me and never uttered a word, even after I did my best to exonerate him. I was as alone as I could be, despite being surrounded by men,

The purpose of our stay in Tahiti was to reprovision the ship with fresh food and water. Tahiti was a perfect location to meet our needs with lush green hills, the dancing waterfalls. The anchorage amongst the coral reefs, and the peaceful natives made this place irresistible, especially to the seamen. Not only did nature share her bounty, but the native girls shared their feminine gifts as well. The crewmen, paddling back and forth from ship to shore gathering game, fruit, wood, and water had ample opportunity to acquaint themselves with the compliant native women. I had to admit; these young women were exceptionally beautiful. The men felt they had landed in an earthly paradise. The Tahitians showed no shame or guilt, no reluctance, and no jealousy about sharing their women. The crewmen were delighted. The idyllic days spent there raised the crew's spirits.

Theirs was a relaxed, more generous sense of ownership, and they assumed our people thought the same way, so they felt free to explore the assortment of sundries on the longboats and carry away any that they wanted. One man, a young adventurous type named Ahutoru, took a particular interest in our ships. Like the other islanders, he swam like fish and had no trouble paddling out to our ships. The crew watched him approach with interest and threw a rope overboard for him. Ahutoru climbed hand over hand, pulling himself up the side of the ship almost effortlessly. He leapt over the rail smiling radiantly and began inspecting this floating village.

If the Tahitian women exemplified feminine allure, Ahutoru was the epitome of male beauty - sturdy, fine-featured, with coppery skin that almost glowed. His hands, arms, and chest displayed ornate tattoos of human forms, turtles, shark teeth and waves. His confident, regal bearing set him apart from the other natives, but unlike some of his fellow islanders, he respected the crew's belongings. He did not paw over them or attempt to pilfer anything. Even so, he was especially curious about every feature of the ship. He carried himself with an air of remarkable self-assurance as he walked among the sailors smiling amiably. He made himself quite at home and soon became a favorite among the crew. He ate with them, marveled at the tall trees that grew from the decks, and displayed a great interest in the agile, monkey-like young men who easily scrambled about far above the deck on a network of ropes. With gestures and facial expressions, he expressed surprise that there were so many men on board, but no women. Cupping his breasts and looking all around he managed to communicate his question: "Where are the women?" The officers responded with a similar pantomime and shook their heads side to side. "No women."

Ahutoru lifted his shoulders to his ears and held his hands palms upward, signaling his question. *"Why not?"*

While the sailors traded nails for fish, crabs, breadfruit, and coconuts, Philibert and I broke free to slip into the jungle to botanize, hoping the crewmen didn't see me. Philibert wanted me with him and believed that I was safe if I was at his side. Clearly, this place was going to be a botanical bonanza, and I was thrilled at the prospect of exploring. Trees with flamboyant flowering vines draped over their branches, and a profusion of glorious red, yellow and orange flowers adorned the hillsides. They were everywhere, proliferating as if this would be their last chance in all eternity to bloom.

And there were trees. Oh, the trees! Tahitians would never go hungry when the coconuts, breadfruit, and bananas were in season. There were banyan trees with canopies spreading like giant umbrellas. We rejoiced to find kapok trees that harbored so much life they were like cities onto themselves. Frogs raised their tadpoles in tiny pools formed by the leaves, vines crawled over their branches, the air roots of epiphytes like orchids and bromeliads dangled from their limbs.

One day, Philibert had wandered off pursuing his own curiosity, while I, with my nose to the ground, immersed myself in examining a pocket of succulents growing in a damp mat of moss. I didn't hear anyone approaching when a pair of strong, ornately tattooed arms gripped me around the waist. My Tahitian captor hoisted me over his well-muscled shoulder as if I weighed less than a bunch of bananas and hurried me off toward the undergrowth. The officer guarding the shore crew pursued him, drew his sword and threatened the kidnapper, who dropped me unceremoniously at his feet. He looked puzzled but shrugged his shoulders and sauntered away. The Tahitians liberally shared their women with us and assumed we would do the same. What strange greedy creatures we were.

Many of our men saw the attempted abduction and by the end of the day everyone had heard about it. I scurried back to our cabin, sat down, rested my arms on my thighs, and hung my head between my knees. Though I'd traveled for over a year with a hundred men who'd grudgingly accepted me as a young man, the Tahitians had seen through my disguise instantly and identified me as a female. Where there had been strong suspicions among the crewmen, now there was certainty.

Ahutoru had made himself at home on the ship and often wandered the decks at night. He leaned against the rail and gazed, enraptured, up at the sky. After the horizon had lost its color, the sky turned the darkest indigo. And while the sailors' attention was diverted by the changing of the watch, I would slip up to the deck unnoticed. Ahutoru began to notice me haunting the deck in the evening, surreptitiously hunkered down among barrels and coiled mounds of rope. He perceived my bleak mood though he did not understand it. At first, he just sat quietly beside me. After a while, he signaled that he wished me to comb his hair. *Really?* I thought, *what an odd request.* He pointed at the Prince of Nassau-Siegen-Siegen-Siegen, standing next to the helmsman on the quarter deck, then pulled and patted his own hair, then pointed at the prince again. *He wanted to look like the handsomest man on board.*

The following night, I smuggled Philibert's fine boar-bristle hairbrush out to the deck and proceeded to comb Ahutoru's thick, black hair. It was long, hanging down the middle of his back to the base of his spine, and a straight as a plumb line. I could not recreate the curls and rolls of the men's wigs, but I plaited it and bound it with a length of twine. He stretched over the rail gazing into the glassy water to see his reflection. He stood, looked at me and grinned ear to ear. "Mauruuru," he said. No doubt this must mean thank you. I smiled back, nodding my head.

Sometimes, he would indicate various items on deck, pointed to my mouth then his own. This curious, clever man wanted to learn our language. He had a great deal of difficulty pronouncing French, but he was bright, and quick-witted, and every day he picked up a few words and phrases. He also made himself well-understood with ingenious sounds and gestures. It wasn't long before he could converse with almost anyone.

He pointed at me and said "mahu," the work word the Tahitians had used to describe me. In his language, it was a term for a man dressed as a woman or vice versa. He was right. That's exactly what I was. He was shocked that cross-dressing would be held against me. In his culture, the 'mahu' people were respected members of the community, neither belittled nor shamed in any way. For me, it meant that I had to hide like a criminal.

On shore, Philibert worked alone or with Prince Nassau-Siegen, collecting specimens for study. Tahitian women and children, eager to help, brought him an assortment of shells, limpets, and plants. Even though my plant gathering had been abruptly cut short, I knew the island abounded with new species, we had not seen before. Why then, I wondered, did Philibert return to the ship with so little to show for his effort. Was he distracted by the women? Did his wound keep him from penetrating too far into the interior? I did not ask. Nor did I criticize or cajole. In addition to bringing back plants, animals, shells, and fish, he traded some unusual shells for several distinctive cloth pieces made from tree bark pounded into rectangles like stiff canvas. I never learned the Tahitian's method of producing this rough fabric, but the samples he collected were beautiful, painted with complex geometrical designs, as well as images of turtles, whales and fish. They were exquisite. If I had been free, I would have bartered for some of these myself. Philibert never offered me any of his, not that I expected him to.

As alluring as Tahiti and its people were, and as much as the men would have enjoyed more time on this island of love, we could not stay for long. When we first landed, Captain Bougainville had met with the local chiefs. Many of them had previous experience with foreigners and knew that eventually they would cause trouble. They did not want Europeans to overstay their welcome and allotted them only ten days. Then they must leave. When the time came, we sailed off with a new passenger, Ahutoru. Bougainville had grown fond of the eccentric Tahitian and took him under his wing. The captain intensified Ahutoru's French lessons, and Ahutoru became increasingly acclimated to European ways. In return, Ahutoru promised he would facilitate communication with other Pacific islanders we might encounter.

Under bluebird skies, we pulled up anchor, left the pristine aquamarine waters of Tahiti behind us, and sailed westward into the uncharted seas of southeast Asia. Guided by Veron's diligent observations of longitude, Captain Bougainville was intent on creating charts of the islands that lay scattered across this vast expanse of ocean. One of the missions of the voyage was to discover a safe route through fluctuating water depths, undulating coastlines and hazardous reefs to map a navigable route that future French colonizers could rely on. If he found fertile land suitable for growing valuable crops, like coffee, or islands with exotic new spices, he would recommend the French create new colonies in those places. Almost two hundred years ago Dutch explorers came home with cloves, mace, nutmeg, cinnamon, and black pepper, and it made them fabulously wealthy. Bougainville hoped to find another pot of gold at the end of his own south Pacific rainbow.

Not long after we left Tahiti, our indefatigable captain fell ill. The *Boudeuse's* surgeon, Monsieur La Port, summoned Philibert to help diagnose the captain's mysterious illness. La Port instructed Philibert to bring whichever of his herbal remedies he thought would treat the captain's particular symptoms.

"You must come with me, Jeanne." Philibert explained. "You are adept at diagnosing symptoms and concocting the best combinations of remedies from the limited assortment we have."

"Of course." I replied simply. I was curious to see the *Boudeuse* but worried that failure to help the captain would make our situation much worse.

I watched with dismay as Philibert descended the rope ladder to the longboat. The crew in the longboat held the ends of the rope ladder tight, but they didn't keep it steady enough for Philibert to climb down, without further injuring his leg. The rope swayed, the longboat bounced on the waves, and the ship rocked, with Philibert clinging desperately to the rope. Philibert yelped and groaned every time his leg smacked or scraped against the hull of *L'Etoile*. By the time he was in position to drop into the longboat, the men were laughing at his graceless misery. I followed, hauling a sturdy sack bulging with ingredients I hoped would be useful in treating the captain's ailment. Philibert was humiliated, his pride injured as much by the men's laughter as his leg. It didn't help that I shimmied down the rope into the longboat as easily as a lizard climbing a wall.

The *Boudeuse's* surgeon, Monsieur La Port, supported Philibert's elbow as he helped him over the rail. La Port was anxious, running his fingers through his thinning, iron-grey hair. He spoke with urgency. "It is not like the sweating disease, but the symptoms are very worrying - fever, chills, severe headache, back pain, general body aches, nausea, vomiting, fatigue, and weakness."

"I understand," said Philibert. "That is a long list, what would make a man suffer from all of them at once is a bit of a mystery. I will confer with my assistant," he said waving the back of his hand in my direction. "We will need a work area."

"Yes, of course," Monsieur demurred, gently guiding Philibert to the surgeon's quarters.

"May I look at the captain?" All heads within earshot swiveled toward me.

"Please excuse him," Philibert reddened with embarrassment. "I agree, a very short examination of the captain would be most helpful."

"Of course," he said though it was clear he was still unsure. "Follow me."

The captain shivered as if cold, but his skin was hot. He didn't have any physical injuries that I could see, but he flailed in his bed barely conscious. "Thank you," Philibert said. "That's enough."

Philibert and I followed Monsieur La Port to the surgeon's quarters where I improvised a concoction of ingredients - holy basil, to decrease inflammation, a honey and garlic mixture to fight fever, chamomile to reduce anxiety and improve sleep, and fennel seeds to protect the heart. Finally, I made a peppermint tea for nausea. I knew these ingredients could treat each symptom individually, but I didn't know what would happen when I combined them. Relief washed over me when we got the news a few days later that the captain had recovered.

Philibert, however, was not as lucky. The scramble up and down the ropes scraped his injured leg raw and made it nearly impossible for him to walk. I went to work once again caring for his seemingly incurable wound.

For two weeks, the sea remained tranquil, and the crewmen relaxed as the ships drifted through calm water like clouds across a peaceful sky. Some enjoyed the respite sitting on the yard arms dangling their legs over the edge, while others enjoyed games of dice and cards on deck. It was a time of plenty – plenty of good luck, good food, good will. Our hold was full, with hundreds of chickens and ducks, pigs, and fresh fruit to keep our bellies full. But it was too good to last.

CHAPTER FOURTEEN

TAHITI TO NEW IRELAND
APRIL TO JUNE 1768

Philibert rested in our cabin for a few days, recovering from the damage done to his injured leg while changing ships. To fill his time, he began sketching and dissecting creatures he'd collected along the way, including a bird, *Rufous hornero*, and dozens of fish. Though their rank smell permeated our cabin, the work diverted his attention from his pain. He had collected dozens of species of wrasse, shimmering with stunning shades of iridescent blue, a cardinal fish whose brilliant yellow body outshone sunflowers. Philibert named a particularly strange creature the bird-mouthed wrasse because its long, thin snout protruded bizarrely, like a bird's beak. He spent a great deal of time describing the frogfish, an ugly creature with warty skin that could change color, used its front fins like feet to walk on the bottom, and a tentacle dangling on its head like a fishing pole to attract prey.

While he occupied himself with these animal species, I examined notes I'd made about the shells, butterflies and plants I collected.

Absorbed in our work as we were, we did not give any thought to our supplies. Apparently, those whose job it was to monitor our food and water supplies didn't give them much thought either. After sitting in barrels for months, since we left Tahiti, our water had become foul. The pigs, poultry, and cows I watched marching up the gangway, had been devoured without any thought of preserving some for leaner times. Fresh fruit does not stay fresh forever, and the coconuts, plantains, and breadfruit we gathered in Tahiti began to rot after a few weeks, adding to the stench in the hold. It was a great waste of food.

Days and weeks passed as we threaded our way through a maze of small islands looking for a place to refresh our provisions. Dark smudges of land appeared on the horizon all around us, but the frothy waves that broke over their protective coral reefs made them unapproachable. The captain had expected to be able to reprovision at one of these islands. There were so many of them, he expected to have his choice of places where we could restock. Instead, we bounced from one island to the next like a billiard ball. At every prospective stop, breakers pounded violently against the shoals shooting spray far into the air.

After two months, the food shortage became acute. The captain ordered an inventory of our remaining food supplies. The officers reported they had enough grain to feed the 400 men on two ships for two-and-a-half months, and enough vegetables for about fifty days, plus a small stock of very old, dried meat. The last pig had been eaten weeks ago. The only other animals left on board our ships were two dogs and a goat.

Occasionally tropical squalls passed over us, and the crew spread tarpaulins across the deck to capture what fresh water we could. Now, instead of enjoying a satisfying meal in the kitchens below deck, everyone, including the officers, found themselves standing in a long line waiting for our daily ration of bread, watery soup, and water.

The ships suffered too. Desiccated planks shrank, sails split, and turned blue with mold. With her mournful groans, *L'Etoile* begged for a safe harbor where she could be repaired, caulked, and treated with oakum. I watched uncounted lush green islands drift by, longing to stop and botanize. Now, our critical mission was to find provisions, and botanizing would only delay us.

After weeks of searching, the lookout spotted an island large enough to warrant exploration. The dream of trading trinkets for fresh food, maybe a pig or some chickens, and clear, healthful water was tantalizing. I started packing up our plant presses, notebooks, and trowels anticipating an accessible landing. Captain Bougainville ordered the ships to lower the longboats and two crews of over thirty officers and scientists, including Philibert and I, climbed in and headed to the island. A delegation of islanders approached us. Prince of Nassau-Siegen, in all his finery, disembarked first, strutting toward them as if he was the reigning monarch. They reacted to the prince as previous natives had done, touching his elaborate clothing, patting and prodding his person.

When the pushing and prodding became too intrusive, he stepped back to maintain a safe distance. The prince made them understand that we had only friendly intentions and were merely looking for food and water. Rustling branches and tittering voices let us know we were being watched. Men and women spied on us from the cover of the dense vegetation. When they understood that we were only looking for food and water, many of them emerged from the bushes and clustered around the landing party. So many in fact, that some of the crewmen got nervous.

The French officers had grown accustomed to being treated well by the natives we encountered. Since these islanders also seemed friendly, the captain felt safe enough to join those on shore. He brought Ahutoru with him to act as translator. A delegation of about ten of our men approached the natives. The natives became agitated, speaking excitedly, waving and gesturing vigorously.

"What are they saying?" the captain asked.

"I don't know, I not speak their language."

"What do you mean? You boasted about how useful you would be as a translator."

"These people are primitives. They speaking language that sounds like animals. I never heard nothing like it. Look at them! Bone through nose they looks like pigs. Is disgusting. Merde!"

Captain Bougainville scanned the crowd. He tended to agree with Ahutoru. These people were as far from the beautiful Tahitians as ash is to water. Their hair was dense and frizzy. Physically, they were short, dark, and repugnant to our eyes. Their skin was pocked and pitted, as if they suffered from a skin disease that looked like leprosy. But that did not matter. Right now, the captain needed their help, and it was Ahutoru's job to communicate with them.

"You must try!" the captain insisted.

"No hope." Ahutoru gestured toward them with a dismissive wave of his hand. "Primitives understand only scare acts. Shoot muskets in air," he pointed to the sky. "Then they do what you say."

"I need you to explain that we need food and water. We will trade with them. We don't need to scare them with our muskets."

Ahutoru stepped closer to the headman sent to greet us. "Need food," he said, and pantomimed eating, "And water." He drank from an imaginary mug. The islanders did not move. No one brought food. Instead, they thumped their long lances on the ground and hooted a full-throated chant.

"This situation is turning hostile." The captain said. "Men, return to the longboats! We are going back to the ships."

Tension crackled in the air like lightning in storm clouds. The crewmen wasted no time, piling back into the longboats to row quickly back to the ships. More islanders emerged, hauling their boats from the underbrush and swarming around our longboats with bows, arrows, and clubs. Startled by the unfriendly confrontation, the crewmen felt intimidated and frightened. The officer in charge of the longboats, a man named Landais, became alarmed. He aimed his gun skyward and shot. A puff of smoke rose into the air. At first the islanders on land were stunned and ran into the woods. But soon they returned with their canoes. Now there were even more boats surrounding us. Landais, convinced he was under attack, decided to return to the ships immediately. The natives' canoes crowded more closely around the longboats as the crewmen tried to retreat. Landais panicked and began shooting. This time he shot to kill.

Despite my frightening experience in Tahiti, I had been excited at the prospect of exploring a new island teeming with new plants. Instead, my excitement turned to horror. I couldn't believe what I was witnessing. It was senseless and brutal, and my heart sank as I watched mayhem and murder erupting around me. I couldn't tell how many natives were killed, but there were several. Our hopes of botanizing on shore were destroyed. More importantly, our hopes of reprovisioning our ships disappeared.

After the tragic fiasco, the captain concluded that whatever chance we had of reprovisioning on this island was gone. The improvident officer, Landais, killed our hopes when he killed the natives. It was now too dangerous to go ashore so we sailed on. We received the same unfriendly reception at the next island we tried. Our only choice was to continue weaving through a maze of unknown islands in hopes of finding a place to anchor so we could at least harvest coconuts, fruits, and wild animals. We passed island after island and found no clear way to approach shore.

Everyone was hungry. Veron, during one of our evening chats on deck, told me that the captain was looking for a place called Quiros

Bay reputed to have good anchorage and supplies, but we found no trace of this bay. Desperation crept over us like the maggots that squirmed in our flour bins.

One by one, the crewmen developed dangerous symptoms. They lost their strength. Men hauling heavy loads who had previously been able to dance through the rigging like monkeys in a tree, sweat glistening on their muscular backs, bare toes curled around the ropes, now staggered through their routine jobs. Nearly everyone became lethargic. Muscles ached; many had bleeding gums, and began to lose their teeth; others sprouted blue or red spots on their skin.

"I have seen this before," Philibert said. "Scurvy has taken hold here. It has been too long since the crew ate fresh food. That trigger-happy idiot, Landais, is to blame for this." Philibert generally ate with the officers, aristocrats and scientists aboard. But now, both of us stood in line with the others waiting for our daily ration of ship's biscuit and whatever other foods the rats had not yet consumed. Soon, the rats themselves were caught and roasted.

I did not complain. Unlike Philibert, I had experienced hunger and knew there was nothing I could do. The sacks that wrapped the food we bought in Montevideo were made of untanned leather. Eventually, in our desperation, we were reduced to cutting the leather into strips, boiling them and eating them. It was like eating shoe leather. Occasionally, the crew caught a small shark or bonito. The cook combined the meager seafood with whatever wilted vegetables were left and served a kind of stew thickened with stale biscuit.

Before the cook boiled the fish though, Philibert would hustle to the ship's galley and insist that he be allowed to fillet the seafood carefully so he would have an intact fish skeleton to analyze. He wrote scientific descriptions of every living thing that was brought aboard.

The hungrier the men got, the more hostile they became toward me. In their minds my presence had brought them bad luck. They felt their irrational hostility was justified by hundreds of years of nautical superstition. They blamed me for our slow starvation. Again, I began carrying one of Philibert's pistols tucked into my waistband wherever I went. As long as I did not appear on deck alone, I felt relatively safe. I hated relying on Philibert to accompany me when I left the cabin, but it was dangerous to walk alone.

Someone had bought two dogs in the Strait of Magellan. The crewmen doted on them, and the canines provided many smiles. But after we had eaten all the coconuts, bananas and assorted vegetables the natives had given us, they too were sacrificed for food. The captain insisted that whatever food remained went first to the men suffering from scurvy. After they were served, there wasn't much left for the rest of us, but the cook made it last as long as possible by imposing a strict rationing system.

Water was an even bigger problem. People can live for weeks without food, but only a few days without water. We economized in every possible way. We washed ourselves and our clothes in salt water. Our stiff clothes cracked and crinkled and chafed and dried our skin. Philibert's wound began oozing pus again, and the persistent rash I developed from binding my chest grew ferocious, redder, and angrier.

Rainfall provided the only fresh water we had, but it was barely enough to keep us alive. Before this disaster descended upon us, I had taken the cook and his work for granted, without thinking too much about it. It didn't occur to me that in order to cook, he needed firewood. Soon wood too was in short supply.

* * *

Many months ago, when suspicion about my gender first became an issue, Captain Giraudais demanded I explain my unusual appearance – why I remained beardless, why I was reluctant to use the heads to relieve myself, why my voice never lowered into a manly register. He remained skeptical about my story, but it was plausible enough, and I was useful as Philibert's caretaker and botanical assistant, so he chose to let it pass. Now, in the throes of hunger, while our progress was slow, and the seas were calm, the issue re-emerged.

While we were becalmed, Captain Bougainville had the opportunity to visit *L'Etoile* to discuss the serious issues of scurvy and starvation, and assess the condition of the ship, the crew, and our remaining food supplies. While on board *L'Etoile,* Captain Bougainville called me to meet him. He demanded an explanation of how I, a woman, wheedled my way on board. I retold my story of being an orphan, (that part at least was true), of being swindled out of my inheritance, and how I decided the best way to earn a satisfactory living was to work as a valet. I told him I tricked Philibert into taking me along as his servant. I pointed out that now Philibert needed more than he ever had. I had diligently served him, not only as a "pack animal," plant collector, and assistant botanist, but also as a nurse and caregiver as his health deteriorated. I tried to answer his questions simply, but I did not apologize for having done an admirable job in all those capacities. After my near abduction in Tahiti, I was no longer passing as a boy, but I was still the loyal helper I had always been.

The captain seemed satisfied with my explanation. I got the impression that he felt he had done his duty investigating the situation, and that was that. He, at least, was willing to show forbearance. Almost no one else shared his tolerant attitude. The crew members grew more hostile by the day, showering me with cat calls, lewd jokes, and threats. Vives stoked the brewing malice against me, insinuating that I was Philibert's 'whore.' I was in constant danger of attack.

* * *

In early June, the *Boudeuse* fired her cannon, a signal to stop immediately and come abreast. The two ships drew close, rocking gently side by side. Everyone gazed out across the great Southern

Ocean. In the middle of this sea what looked like an enormous sand bar emerged. It stretched for so many miles we could not see where it ended. The waves lapped at it, covering then uncovering a mysterious bank of green rock. Both captains inspected it through their telescopes. Those of us on deck gawked at what appeared to be mounds of moss as green as jade. Countless numbers of birds perched on the rocks - gannets, petrels, and boobies alighted, launched, and swirled above us their screeches creating a thunderous din.

"It's a coral shoal," Philibert said. "We've seen small reefs around many islands, but the size of this one is staggering." His pointed finger tracked across a wall of green rock as far as the eye could see. "We have not seen green coral before, but regardless of its color, I'm sure it could rip the hull to pieces. To you it might look like a spectacle of nature, but to me it looks like a ship's graveyard."

The captain and his officers reached a consensus that proceeding through this snarl of reefs would be too dangerous. The voyage had come this far, and it would be a tragedy to risk all we had accomplished trying to push through the largest coral reef any of them had ever seen. With that door closed to us, on June sixth the captain steered a northeasterly course heading toward New Guinea. We knew we were getting closer to land when we began to see floating logs bobbing in the water. It was a hopeful sign. We needed wood to feed the cook's ovens but retrieving the jagged driftwood was treacherous. Some of the bravest, or most foolhardy men took up the challenge. They secured themselves to the boat with long ropes wrapped around their waists, slithered down ropes into the water, laid hold of the first timber, and dragged it back to the ship. Deck hands on board coordinated their efforts calling "heave ho" in unison and hauled the water-logged trunks onto the deck. By late afternoon, five large logs lay dripping at their feet on board. A round of spirited back slapping relieved the intense anxiety.

I awoke one morning to the sound of rain pattering on the deck. What a blessing! Weeks ago, when it was apparent the drinking water had gone bad, I squirreled a wine carafe away in our cabin. I would never have thought that a carafe of water could bring such joy. What should I use it for? Should I swallow it down? Wash my crusty clothing? Clean Philibert's suppurating wound? It was a good problem to have. A little for him and a little for me – neither of us got much, but it helped.

CHAPTER FIFTEEN

NEW IRELAND
MAY TO JUNE 1768

Philibert took solace in the unswerving confidence he had in the captain. He began taking his meals with the officers, while I waited in the cabin for him to bring my portion. One evening, he returned from his meal looking dejected.

"He doesn't know what to do. He knows how desperate our situation is, but from the first day of the voyage, he believed we would surely to find food, water, and wood somewhere among the south sea islands. He had not anticipated hostility from the natives, nor the danger presented by these hideous coral reefs."

That miscalculation led to our current extreme circumstances. One look around the ship confirmed the serious deterioration of the ship and the suffering seamen. We were all dejected, and weak with hunger.

"The captain will keep trying to find a place where we can land and find food, water, and wood. What choice does he have?" I didn't know whether I was trying to comfort Philibert or myself. I wasn't sure I believed my own words.

Three more times we attempted to land and all three times the coral fortresses repelled us. Whenever the captain deployed the longboats to investigate a likely landing place, small armadas of fierce warriors surrounded our crews, aiming sturdy bows at the men, and brandishing long, menacing pikes, weapons they would happily use if we came any closer. I couldn't help but admire the extraordinary craftsmanship of their beautiful vessels. Gracefully curved bows and sterns, ornamented with meticulously carved figureheads. Some even hoisted a sail. It was dangerous to be on deck during these encounters, but my curiosity overcame my good sense.

I took cover on deck and watched as the natives approached our vessels. The people of these south sea islands lacked anything we would call civilization. They were naked, their bodies and hair painted white all over, but they were masterful of navigators and deftly maneuvered their well-built scows around us blocking any approach to their islands. They certainly did not lack bravery or strength. Twice, when our seamen didn't turn around quickly enough, they launched arrows over their heads as a warning.

After being thwarted repeatedly, the captain shifted to a northeasterly course, and, within a few weeks, the island of New Guinea rose above the horizon. Tier upon tier of rocky palisades rose steeply from beach to tropical rainforest to subalpine meadows.

The island was glorious, and I was certain it would yield an abundance of exotic plants. We got so close that we could smell the perfume of the lush vegetation. Landing, however, again proved impossible. For several days, heavy fog covered the forests, the sea, and the ships. There were times when those standing on the rear deck could barely see the bow. Fluctuating offshore winds drove our ships backward, then forward, then back again. We couldn't hold our position long enough to make a landing. My disappointment felt like a physical blow, and my stomach growled like an angry dog.

On July sixth we entered a narrow strait running between two long, low, fertile islands.

The island to the south was called New Britain, the one to the north was New Ireland. These were on the captain's maps, so he was finally certain where we were. The passage was so narrow it blocked the worst of the winds, and the steady flow of water through the passage kept it free from countercurrents or whirlpools. The ships finally found an anchorage in Port Praslin, a sizeable harbor on the island of New Ireland. Captains, officers, crew and civilians – everyone rejoiced. Finally, we would drink clear water, eat fruit, native vegetables, and hopefully find some edible wildlife larger than the ships' rats.

Every man strong enough to haul tents and equipment to shore happily pitched camp. With solid land beneath their feet and clean land air that did not stink of oakum, mold, and vinegar, our desperation lifted. The ships needed as much rehabilitation as the crew. The pebbly beach provided enough room to haul the ships ashore. Carpenters, joiners, and tars set to work repairing the damage inflicted by rough seas.

It was a splendid spot. Mysteriously, for all its beauty, it appeared to be uninhabited. Flotillas of hostile, well-armed islanders did not paddle out to threaten us here. White-painted aborigines did not pound their pikes on the ground to drive us away.

Servants, like me, had plenty of work. No one had washed their clothes properly since Tahiti, so several of us took this opportunity to do laundry. The servants were a motley crew, but since they were employed by gentlemen, they were less uncouth than the crewmen. Some were well past their prime, having been with their masters for many years, and some were mere boys perhaps ten or eleven years old. They formed a kind of fraternity, not part of the rabble of deck hands, but not far enough up the ladder to merit special treatment. I kept a good distance from them as I squatted on the beach washing, rinsing and washing again our shirts, undergarments, stockings and pants. I raised my head from my work and watched forlornly as Philibert wandered off without me looking for shells and plants.

I concentrated on my chore, head down, pistols tucked into my waistband, not paying much attention to the other servants. Gradually, the murmur of casual conversation was punctuated by outbursts of hilarity and shouting, like men drinking in an alehouse. Vives' high, whiney voice rose above the babble, and his tone changed from good-natured claptrap to a hostile grumble. I didn't think much of it. Then, without warning, one of the servants grabbed me from behind, curling one arm around my neck in a chokehold, violently twisting my other arm behind my back. I squirmed and kicked, jerking violently trying to break his grip. Three others joined him; one took my free arm, and two others grabbed my legs. They picked me up and swept me into the forest so quickly I had no chance to escape. They dropped me and flattened me against the ground. Tree roots dug into my back; my hair tangled and clotted in the shrubs. They pulled my pistols from my waistband and pointed them at my face. A heavy hand pressed against my mouth. The hands of those not restraining me, ripped off my shirt, and tore off my bindings. Other hands tugged at my pants and yanked them off. The young men who held my feet spread them apart. My terror was indescribable. I felt my spirit drift away from my body. I had the sensation I was looking down on the scene from a above. *"I am going to die here,"* I thought.

Through the fog of horror, I heard a young but commanding voice. "Do you know what the penalty for rape is?" it said. I recognized this voice, but I couldn't place it. *Who is that?* Then I remembered the young man I spoke to on the beach at La Rochelle. *It's Etienne,* I thought. *It's the timekeeper's assistant.*

"You've gotten what you came for," he continued, speaking loudly with the voice of authority. "Look! Look at her! Yes, he's a girl. Now you know. You'd better let her go."

"You think I'm going to stop now?" A guttural voice crackled like bacon grease in a pan, hot and sputtering. I could practically hear the saliva dribbling from his lips. This was one of those men who enjoyed tripping me and pushing me into the rail, laughing at me as I maneuvered around him.

"You'd better stop now. All of you! Have a good look. Have you never seen a woman before?" Some of them were young enough that they probably hadn't. "Our captains are honorable men. They will defend this girl's honor, and they will not defend yours, because you have none."

The frenzy abated. The whooping and laughing died down. Slowly, one by one, they turned their backs and shuffled back to the beach. A few kicked dirt at me as they left. Etienne reached out a hand and pulled me to my feet. "Get dressed," he said. "This is not over. They will try to harm you again if they can. You'd better stay in your cabin, or at least not wander around on your own." He handed the pistols back to me. "Now get out of here." He turned his back and left.

I stood, reeling. I tried to thank him, but words would not form. I staggered back to the beach, stumbling over roots, breathing in short gasps, my entire body shaking as if I was freezing. Philibert emerged from the undergrowth and found me huddled over the wet clothing.

"Philibert! The servants!" I cried. "As I was washing clothes on the beach, the other servants ambushed me and dragged me away. Vives laughed and goaded them on, They, they . ."

"What? What did they do?" Philibert demanded tersely.

"They ripped off my bindings and pulled down my trousers." I was so mortified by shame I couldn't look at Philibert as I spoke.

"Did they violate you?" Philibert asked in voice as cold as ice water in winter.

"No. But they wanted to. They inspected me, as they would an animal. I felt sure I was going to die, right there on the beach. Etienne, the timekeeper's apprentice discovered the scene unfolding and reminded them what their punishment would be if they raped me."

Philibert was silent for a long time. Waves of competing emotions washed across his face - shock, anger, fear, disgust. I expected some gesture of consolation, a pat on the arm or a word of sympathy. But Philibert offered neither.

"Do you realize how this will reflect on me? If the captain believes I knowingly brought a woman on board, my career will end in disgrace. Though you told me you convinced him I was innocent, and that you tricked me, I will still be blamed."

"Is that all you have to say?"

"No. When we leave here, you will go back to our tent and stay there until we leave. In the future, you will go exploring only in my presence." He addressed me as if I was an errant child.

"I wasn't exploring! I was washing your dirty linen!" I whipsawed from mortification to wild rage and wanted to rip out every hair on his balding head. "Feel free to wash your own laundry. Be my guest!"

I struggled to gain control of myself as I followed Philibert back to the camp. With every step, I detested him more. That night, I tried to console myself with the thought that all was not lost. With Philibert, I could still indulge in my greatest pleasure, discovering new and exotic wonders in remote places at the ends of the earth. All I had to do was follow him around like the lackey I was. I allowed myself one night of misery, indulging in self-pity and anger. In the morning, I stowed my trauma away in the vault in my heart where I kept my saddest memories and did not dwell on them again.

* * *

After the detestable incident, I sequestered myself in our tent. Even with my pistols tucked into my waistband I did not feel safe. Anxiety robbed me of my sleep. Next time they came for me, I would be ready. I wouldn't threaten. I'd shoot to kill. I didn't care if they hanged me for murder. If that was the price of my honor, so be it.

As though it was for him to decide, Philibert concluded that I had spent enough time recovering. He woke me in the mornings and insisted I go foraging with him. I followed dutifully and soon the forest absorbed all my attention. The balled fist of fear loosened its grip on my heart.

For several days it rained. I mean it *really* rained. Torrential downpours hammered our camp mercilessly and gale-force winds threatened to hurl our tents into the sea. When the storm had wrung itself out, the world was even more opulent. Glittering droplets clung to every surface. Spider webs drooped with tiny diamond beads.

The beach where we camped was beautiful beyond all reason. If an artist were to draw this place, no one would believe this vision was of this earth. Waterfalls poured from the cliffs to the beach. Though water was abundant, the captain decided how it was to be used. He designated the water of the nearest fall be used by the men from the *Boudeuse,* the second for *L'Etoile's* crew, and the third he set aside for bathing. The abundance of water was an easily accessible blessing, but it was a struggle to haul the all-important timber to the shore.

Everyone from the ships' boys to the aristocrats enjoyed combing the beach for fascinating little treasures. There was an endless variety of shells - giant clams, conches, cones, augers, cowries shaped like perfect cones or spirals. Even Captain Bougainville brought his most unusual finds to Philibert to be classified and named.

The cornucopia of bananas, coconuts, papayas, and other tropical delicacies that we expected to find, however disappointed us. It was not the season for ripened fruit, and the immature samples provoked terrible stomach pains and diarrhea. Whatever edible plants we found went to the scurvy victims first. Their lethargy improved somewhat once they were off the ship, breathing healthful land air. But their gums were so spongy, porous and bleeding they lost teeth; and the gaps made it hard for them to eat. Their breath reeked intolerably. Their legs swelled and eventually erupted with fetid ulcers.

A coterie of hunters dispatched by the captain thrashed through the bushes searching for wild boars, nightmarish creatures, with powerful bodies, spikey fur, and a distinctly aggressive disposition. The mature males sprouted intimidating curving tusks they put to good use viciously protecting their families.

"What do you suppose wild boars eat?" I asked Philibert.

"The hunters swear they can hear them grunting as they root about for tubers on the slopes above. They say they've seen evidence of their presence in shallow holes where they dug out cassava," he replied.

"Can you ask the hunters to bring some of them back to camp? The scurvy victims need more plant food, and I see no reason the native tubers would not help them recover."

With a simple nod of agreement from Philibert the hunters brought back the much-appreciated fresh roots. The scurvy didn't disappear, but most of the men improved noticeably.

Very few animals grew large enough to hunt, apart from birds. A huge assortment of beautiful birds glided through the forests. To me they seemed far too lovely to hunt, but hunt them they did, with paltry results. The birds took one look at the muskets and disappeared into dense thickets. Only the odd, ground-dwelling cassowaries failed to evade the hunters. It was unfathomable that such a lush, prolific environment, bursting with diversity, would produce such meager results.

After my hyper-vigilant anxiety abated, my natural curiosity overtook me once again and I enjoyed roaming the island from the brushy coastal scrub to forests high in the hills, always with Philibert and never alone. Though he was slow and suffered chronic pain from his never-healing wound, I stayed within sight of him. Our botanizing excursions were blessedly productive. We reveled in finding new species more diverse than I could ever have imagined – towering trees whose branches grew like flat dinner plates perched on the top of conical trunks, giant coconuts so hard the shells had to be hammered open. But once exposed, the huge nuts yielded delicious milk in addition to meaty white flesh. Creepers like trumpet vines writhed up trunks. Orchids clung to high branches, dangling roots that drew sustenance from the air itself. Ferns grew on the tops of trees. I was dizzy with delight exploring the tropical forests and shrubby beaches.

Somehow, we would need to find more room in our cabin for all our specimens, even though it was already overcrowded with thousands of species gleaned from every landfall we'd made. We labeled each one with its own tiny card bearing its Latin name, its vernacular name, and when and where it had been collected. Hour upon hour, I buried myself in the work. When each was properly cataloged, I lovingly mounted them between two flat boards lined with absorbent paper, squeezed them tightly, then hung them in orderly rows in the crates the ship's carpenter designed for us. Even though the captain's quarters were the largest available on the ship, it was too small. There was only enough room remaining to collect species that were new to us, or never-before recorded by science. Nourished by the miraculous abundance of the natural world - ferns, mosses, flowers and birds - I buried my trauma, resentments, and sorrow and allowed my soul to heal.

We enjoyed great success botanizing, but the hunters killed few animals large enough to eat. There were large bats that darted wildly at very high speed, but it was nearly impossible to hold them in the sights of a gun long enough to shoot. Rats rustled around in the debris on the forest floor, but the sailors, who had already eaten so many rats, ate them only as a last resort. The fish were small and colorful, but and hidden in the crevices of coral reefs. The abundant fruits we hoped for were still green and bitter. Everyone - crew, officers, civilians, and scientists alike - was almost as hungry and desperate as ever. A diet of mostly under-ripened fruit was not enough to sustain three hundred men. Scurvy was still taking its toll with bleeding gums, ghoulish skeletal bodies, and lethargy born of starvation. The men's clothing was as tattered as the wind-ravaged sails. I counted myself fortunate that I was skilled enough with needle and thread to spare Philibert and me the indignity of wearing clothes that were falling to ruin.

CHAPTER SIXTEEN

DUTCH EAST INDIES
AUGUST TO SEPTEMBER 1768

Captain Bougainville stared glumly at the officers from both ships - the first mates, navigators, the scientists and the cartographer. They sat in somber silence, facing each other across a heavy oak table securely nailed to the floor. Everyone knew the captain was a proud man who jealously protected his precious reputation. The seamen spoke of him in hushed tones with utmost respect. He had clearly demonstrated his sense of fairness and his genuine concern for the crew by standing in line with his men for his ration of stale biscuit and nearly inedible dried meat. He felt responsible for having led his crew, wracked by disease and starvation, into this crisis. The weight of his culpability showed in his rounded shoulders and the loose fit of his threadbare uniform. It had been his decision to rely on finding sustenance among the islands of the South Pacific, but his strategy had been a dismal failure.

"We have been on this beach for twenty days, and our men are as desperately hungry as ever. We need to find help." He scanned the dour-faced men before him seeing dismay, sadness, and desperation. "As humiliating as it is, our best course of action is to find the nearest European settlement, where at least we will find food." He straightened and spoke more loudly. "You may see it as weakness, but saving my men is more important that maintaining my pride. I have decided to head for the Dutch islands of the East Indies."

"But Captain," the ship's engineer spoke up. At sixty-two, the grizzled veteran of many voyages had seen more risky decisions and their dire consequences than any of the others. "The Dutch have held power in the spice islands for over two hundred years."

"Believe me, I have searched my soul over this decision." Bougainville shook his head and looked down at the table, then took a deep breath. "Throwing myself on the mercy of the Dutch will be a personal disgrace, but I have no other choice."

"But Captain," Vives waved his fist in the air as if winding up to punch someone.

"Stop! Would you rather see your fellow seamen die? I will not sacrifice their lives for the sake of my honor."

Vives lowered his hand. The men exchanged soul searching gazes. One by one each of them nodded. That evening, when Philibert recounted the meeting to me, I could visualize him meekly assenting.

"You did the right thing supporting the captain's decision." I placed a consoling hand on his shoulder. "There was no other choice."

At the end of July, we left New Ireland. Somewhere among the bewildering maze of islands that was the south Pacific were the hoped-for European saviors. The islanders in these waters had dealt with the Dutch for one hundred and fifty years, gaining sufficient experience with Europeans to know that foreigners could not be trusted, and their intentions were anything but friendly. During all that time the Dutch maintained a strangle-hold on the spice trade and the natives forced to serve them. Therefore, as soon as they sighted our tall ships, the islanders sent their boats out to threaten us and drive us away. If the Dutch discovered them trading with anyone else, the consequences would be drastic and bloody. Therefore, conflict with other Europeans was almost inevitable. Because both sides expected violent confrontation, that's what they got. Relationships with the natives were so bad that Captain Giraudais took to firing upon anyone who came too close to the ships, increasing the level of hostility even further.

The Dutch held an absolute monopoly over trading in their territory. Since 1602 when the Dutch established the East India Company, they had ingeniously limited the production of spices. Cloves thrived on one tiny island, nutmeg on another; and cinnamon grew only in the Moluccas. If any enterprising trader tried to plant or sell these spices, he would soon find his plantation engulfed in the flames. If any islanders were caught selling to anyone but the Dutch, the European monopolists had no compunctions about attacking them. The Hollanders jealously guarded the location of their spice islands, refusing to share maps or nautical advice with any foreigner. The islands were a maze of tiny, scattered keys governed by contrary currents, and impenetrable coral reefs.

Nevertheless, as he cruised through the islands, Captain Bougainville remained alert for new locations where crops might be grown for good profit. Coffee, for instance, was gaining popularity in Europe. Plantations could be very lucrative so he kept a sharp eye out for unsettled islands that might support French immigrant colonies.

Philibert and I were useful once again. Whenever the longboats could get to shore, the captain eagerly sent us out to survey the possibilities. That was one of the main reasons Philibert was appointed to this voyage in the first place. With few maps and very little geographical information at his disposal, the captain veered south where he hoped to locate the island of Batavia and the larger island of Ceram. If he located those islands, he could orient himself on his maps.

Bougainville concocted the ploy of running the Dutch flag up the mast to lure the natives' boats toward us so we could trade for food and supplies. It backfired completely. The Dutch had been so heavy handed that the islanders fled at first sight of the Dutch flag. In an atmosphere fraught with fear and mistrust, we could hardly expect to find cooperative locals with whom to trade. They would not come near us, and we could not go ashore in Dutch territory without permission. The captain finally decided to drop anchor offshore a short distance from a plantation on the island of Buru. There he would wait for the Dutch authorities to come to us. A French-speaking administrator finally came on board to ask why we were in his territory.

"Quite simply," Bougainville began. "We are starving. Our supplies have all been consumed or have rotted. It has been months since the crew has eaten more than half rations of vermin-infested ship's biscuit and dried meat." Bougainville's shoulders sank, and his expression pinched with shame. He swept an arm toward his tattered, emaciated crew. "Just look at them."

"Are you quite sure your mission is not espionage? Because if you try to abscond with any of our spices, you will pay in blood and any men who survive will continue to starve."

"No, sir. Our mission is to scout for new lands unclaimed by any other European power. We have no intention of stirring up a hornet's nest with territorial disputes."

The official scanned the crew's sunken eyes and skeletal bodies, and his demeanor softened. "You and your officers will dine with us tonight."

"Thank you, sir. We would be honored."

I watched from the deck with the other servants and sailors, all of us ravaged by harrowing hunger, as Philibert and the other officers walked off the ship to their first proper supper in months. Anticipating a real meal made our mouths water and our stomachs growl. Food - fresh food - reached us the following day. Never had a bowl of rice, a small fish, and an apricot tasted so good. Seamen, who always strongly favored meat over any other food, devoured the fish as greedily as if it was a fat slab of beef, and the vegetables as if they were candy.

A cadre of Dutch officials examined the ships, searching for contraband. Our cabin attracted special scrutiny. They poked through every crate, investigated every specimen hanging to dry, and probed every corner and cranny of our quarters. When they found nothing but wild plants in which they had no interest at all, the officials agreed to let us go ashore and resume our search.

The smell of fresh air was nature's own medicine. Despite the constant scrutiny of the Dutch overseers who accompanied us everywhere, the feel of solid land beneath my feet brought true joy. It was the first time anyone other than my shipmates had laid eyes on me since the fiasco on New Ireland. And what a sight I was! Since my humiliation, I had not bothered with my bindings, yet I still wore the baggy pants, and loose blouse of an ordinary seaman for the simple reason that I had brought no women's clothes with me. A fog of anxiety hung over me like a thunder cloud. I had good reason to fear, but I struggled to put those worries aside, determined to hold my head up. I wasn't going to be foolhardy either. I stayed by Philibert's side as he peppered our chaperones with questions about the plants and animals of the island of Buru, deliberately annoying them enough that they kept their distance from the feisty, officious little Frenchman, while continuing to observe our every move.

During our week at the plantation, the quartermaster bought everything we needed to restock our supplies from the planter.

"They are taking advantage of our circumstances." Philibert grumbled. "They are charging exorbitant prices."

"We are so far away from any other island, and they need to feed themselves too," I tried to defend our saviors. "Here we are, begging from a Dutch plantation owner who has no obligation to help us. We should be grateful." Philibert stopped complaining.

The scurvy victims improved markedly when they began to eat regular meals, drink clean water, soak up sun, and breathe healthful land air. Our time on Buru was not nearly long enough for us to catalog the wondrous variety of species we found there. The island was so far away from anywhere else; it would take a lifetime to catalog the astounding number of unique birds, butterflies, and plants that lived on this island alone, and nowhere else on earth.

Extravagantly colored birds glided among the exotic trees. Dozens of varieties of parakeets, large and small, created a din that echoed through the trees. The tiny dwarf kingfisher and purple breasted monk bird defied the imagination with a dozen colors splashed over their little bodies. I learned there were animals that carried their under-developed young in sacs outside their bodies. It was charming and absurdly amusing to see their little faces poking out from their mother's pouches. Huge bats, called flying foxes, with enormous wings as wide as the tallest man swooped silently through the forests. If anyone had described these species to me before I saw Buru, I would have thought they were liars.

After a week we left Buru, well provisioned with rice, dried venison, fish, cattle, a few hens, and full barrels of fresh water. Our stay was far too brief to do the natural majesty of the place justice, but the captain decided it was time for us to continue. Of all the heavenly places we visited so far, Buru would live in my memory as the land that saved our lives. When we departed, the captain wisely employed a local guide who knew how to navigate the shoals and safely escort us through the jumble of islands. Our South Pacific idyl cleansed me of almost two years' worth of anxiety. I felt like myself again.

On September twenty-eighth, the dome of the Dutch Calvinist church on the island of Batavia came into view, and we anchored again. This place was not a secluded plantation nor a wild, uncharted island. It was a full-fledged town, built as a trading post by the Dutch in 1610. An ingenious canal system encompassed the city forming a ring around its center like an orderly grid of roads, but on water rather than on land. Crude houses sprawled beyond the canals, and beyond the residential neighborhoods stretched miles of farmland. The shore festered amid all manner of decaying refuse, as it did in most of the towns. Sewage filled the muddy canals. Ramshackle huts in various states of disrepair slumped along the shore.

Sailors slithered through the squalor as if born to it, sniffing out the rancid odor of their typical diversions - fallen women and strong drink. They indulged themselves until they became sick with dysentery, diarrhea, and gonorrhea, diseases that festered on the swampy shores. The contrast between the degradation of Batavia and the paradise of Tahiti or Buru could not have been greater if we had landed on the moon. Beyond the degradation, away from the city, I was certain unsullied nature reigned in glory and broad swaths of wildflowers scented the air.

It would have been suicide for me to prowl this town alone, so I remained on board with Philibert's pistol tucked into my waistband. Philibert and the Prince of Nassau-Siegen, had no such strictures, and climbed the surrounding slopes where the estates of rich planters and traders flourished. I couldn't help seething with envy when Philibert and the prince returned from their explorations, bubbling over with vivid descriptions of sugar and rice plantations, surrounded by apricot trees. I retreated into my shell like the great turtles we sighted on the shores of South America.

I toiled away, diligently labeling, categorizing and storing our growing library of plant specimens, as I had been doing for almost two years. I was not sorry when, in mid-October after about a month on Batavia, we sailed on.

From this point onward, the voyage home was well-charted, and Captain Bougainville considered his mission to discover, map, and explore a route through the Indies had been achieved. His attention now shifted to rounding the horn of Africa and speedily returning to France. Only two stops, one on the Ile de France and another on the Cape of Good Hope, remained. The seamen anxiously anticipated seeing home again, to reunite with loved ones and families they hadn't seen for two years.

A few weeks into the final leg of our voyage, the first mate discovered a tawdry bunch of French deserters stowed away among the barrels and boxes in the hold. They had snuck on board in Batavia, unnoticed amid the customary flurry of activity that accompanied the loading of the ships.

The first mate created quite a scene when he hauled this motley bunch up the gangway to face the captain on deck. Captain Giraudais stood stiffly, as the mates dragged five men by their scruffy necks and tossed them at the captain's feet.

"These men were found crouching among the casks and chests in the hold."

Giraudais' face reddened with rage. "Who are you? What are you doing here?"

The men groveled, cowering on their knees, their hands tied behind their backs. One man raised his head and spoke. His filthy black hair hung in clotted masses over his dark eyes. The skin that covered his skeletal body was so grimy it was impossible to tell his natural color. "I am Louis Renard, sir. The ship I was on left port without me."

"You mean you were too drunk to drag yourself on board at the appointed time."

The man's shoulders slumped forward, and he did not reply. One by one, each of them explained the circumstances that had left him marooned on Batavia.

"Do you know the penalties for stowing away on His Majesty's ship?" He did not wait for a reply. "Well let me tell you. I could have you stripped naked, lashed to the mast and beaten bloody. I could maroon you on an uninhabited island. I could throw you overboard." He drew himself up, took a deep breath, and looked down on the filthy lot of them. One of the wretches tried to crawl away, only to be kicked viciously by one of the seamen who dragged him back to his place at the captain's feet.

"Captain," the first mate spoke up. "May I have a word?" Giraudais and the mate walked to the quarter deck out of earshot. "Sir, we have lost seven men to disease, and several others are still too ill to work. It seems these leeches have some experience on ships. They are French and trying to make their way back to their home country. We could place them with a military regiment when we reach Mauritius, if the captain there accepts them. If not, they can be put ashore there. In the meantime, perhaps we could put them to work. Since we must feed them anyway, we might as well reap some benefit from their labor."

"I suppose you are right. Put them to work." His rage subsided.

When they returned to the main deck, Captain Giraudais gave his orders. "Tie them to the mast. Give each of them ten lashes and then douse them with sea water."

The first mate paused, knowing the sting of saltwater against flayed skin, but the circumstances left no room for mercy.

"Carry on," the captain ordered, then turned and walked away.

Most of the crewmen watched the lashing stoically, but some of them enjoyed the spectacle, laughing at each scream of pain. Captains at sea had complete authority over discipline and many enforced order with a merciless vigor. Giraudais and Bougainville, however, had thus far never needed to resort to severe measures. After the whipping, the stowaways were ordered to clean themselves up and were put to work. Eventually the crew accepted them, and the stow-aways caused no further trouble.

Cheers rang out among the crew when, after nearly two years, we finally reached the French territory of Ile de France. Inspired by their success, they sang with gusto - "Alors, leve ton verre" - All right! Lift your glass." The governor, Intendent Pierre Poivre, stood smiling on the quay as he waited to welcome his old friend Philibert Commerson.

The sweet tones of spoken French were music to our ears. Though the faces we saw were white, black, and brown the language they spoke was French. After twenty-two months sailing from one foreign land to another, our feet finally touched French soil. It felt like home.

CHAPTER SEVENTEEN

ILE DE FRANCE and PAMPLEMOUSSE
1768

Welcome to Ile de France." A tall, handsome, middle aged man with sympathetic eyes and pert cupid's bow lips, stepped forward smiling broadly. He turned and bowed toward Captain Bougainville and Captain Giraudais. "I am delighted to extend my hospitality to you."

"Thank you for hosting us. We will reprovision swiftly and be on our way," Captain Bougainville replied. "We do not wish to impose on your generosity."

Then he faced Philibert. He grasped Philibert's hand with both of his, pumping it heartily. "It's hard to believe that two years ago, in far off Paris, both of us were preparing for our separate missions, yours to circle the globe and discover new species, and mine to take up my post here in Ile de France as administrator. And now, in this remote corner of the globe, here we are, together again."

Philibert smiled wanly. "My dear Monsieur Poivre," he said, extending his hand to shake. "It's quite remarkable that our paths have crossed again. We have so much to catch up on. I heard you have built an impressive botanical garden here."

Monsieur Poivre took a step backward and gave Philibert an appraising glance. What he saw was a man sobered by experience. The paths of these two men had first crossed in Paris. At that time Monsieur Poivre, was already a successful trader and merchant. He had heard about the famous botanist of the Jardin de Roi during a short visit in Paris. The rumor was that Philibert was gregarious, and enthusiastic, if a bit irascible, and that he had great ambitions to become a famous botanist, respected by his countrymen and the scientific community. The man he saw before him was thin, angular, with pain etched across his face, deflated like a sail on a windless sea.

"I can't tell you how happy I am to be here." Philibert could feel the weight of Poivre's appraising gaze and wanted it to end. He squared his shoulders and stood as erect as he could. "I look forward to comparing our experiences. I have collected thousands of specimens during this long voyage."

"As have I," Monsieur Poivre replied. "I can't wait to show you my collections and my estate."

The men wandered off, and I trailed after them. Unsurprisingly, Poivre took no notice of me. I was totally unremarkable, dressed as a boy, as shabby as any of the other crew members. He did not recognize me, but I recognized him. In 1766, when I lived with Philibert in Paris as his house servant, Pierre and Philibert's paths crossed at the Jardin de Roi. One serene summer Paris night, I catered a soiree Philibert had arranged for the notables from the Jardin. Poivre was in Paris for a short time before he was sent to Ile de France to become the island's Intendent, the chief administrator. Around the same time, Philibert was appointed King's Botanist for the upcoming voyage of circumnavigation. Poivre didn't take note of me then or now. Why would he? I was only a servant. But I remember his enthusiasm when he pledged to establish a museum of botany on the other side of the world.

"I would be honored to have you stay at my residence, Le Chateau Mon Plaisir," Monsieur Poivre offered. "It is spacious enough for your collection, and I can provide a well-appointed apartment for you."

"That sounds ideal. I appreciate your generosity. With a name like Mon Plaisir, how could it fail to be lovely?" Philibert made a vain attempt at cheerfulness.

"I too am an ardent botanist and naturalist. I have collected innumerable plant specimens and identified hundreds of new species here on Ile de France. And I have barely scratched the surface. I am building a large botanic garden on the grounds of my estate. If I am successful, it will be one of the best in the world. We have much to discuss." He glanced at me. An ambiguous flicker of uncertainty flashed across his face and quickly passed. "Feel free to bring your servant with you."

"Thank you for your generosity. My assistant has been most helpful to me, and I have grown to trust his attention to detail and meticulous record keeping. He is also vigorous and strong and can clamber over rough terrain that my leg wound prevents me from exploring."

"Very well, then. We will find a comfortable room for him in the servant's quarters."

* * *

The next few weeks transformed my life once again. The following morning, I awoke in my own small but comfortable room, in a feather bed, nestled among soft pillows. *This is what heaven must feel like.* I thought. I ate a delicious and plentiful breakfast provided by our generous host. I wore clean clothing. Yes, it was still men's clothing, but at least I did not smell of salt, tar, and vinegar.

Port Louis on the Island of Ile de France was at the heart of a thriving international market, throbbing with the vigorous heartbeat of commerce. Goods from east and west changed hands among a diverse community of traders. White Europeans, brown islanders, and black men, many of them escaped slaves, crowded streets lined with low-slung wooden houses, crouching behind tall fences. Though it lay in a pleasant enough setting at the seaward end of a valley surrounded by high mountains, it was an austere, utilitarian port town, and little had been done to beautify it. No trees lined the rough caliche streets, no flowers adorned the squat houses, no parks or public spaces enhanced the town, but it was on solid ground that did not heave beneath my feet; and that was a relief.

* * *

During out first days in Ile de France, Captain Bougainville focused his attention on offloading anything that would slow his speedy return to France. No longer worried about being attacked in the streets, I watched as scores of men on stretchers were taken from our ships to the island's hospital.

Bougainville called Philibert to his quarters for a private audience. "I have come to the conclusion that you will be useful here on Ile de France. I hereby dismiss you from the King's service,"

Philibert was stunned. His stomach lurched, his muscles went rigid, and his posture stiffened. "May I ask why you have come to this decision?"

"Yes, you may. You have outlived your usefulness to this voyage," he pronounced so coldly Philibert could hardly believe he was the same man. "If you want to write about your findings, you can easily accomplish that from here. This is French territory. If you wish to return to France in the future, you may do so. I have not singled you out to punish you. Several others will also be remaining here. Several others are no longer needed. Two pilots will stay behind, as will the chaplain. I have had this conference with him also, and he does not mind staying behind, because he believes he can tend to the spiritual needs of the city. The hospital will be stocked with all the medicines I no longer need. And there are certainly plenty of ill and injured men who will benefit from hospital care. And since the island is growing in importance, I will leave it under the protection of a platoon of soldiers. Veron the astronomer is happy to stay behind to complete his important astronomical work."

A sudden coldness hit Philibert at his core. He was longer essential for a quick return to France, so he was being jettisoned. It was logical that Veron would gladly stay behind to continue his work. With the information he had already learned, he intended to accurately measure the width of the Pacific Ocean for the first time. This alone would be a great leap forward for seamen who were sometimes forced to use only dead reconning to find their way to distant ports. Here in Ile de France, he had a new project. He wanted to be on land to track the transit of Venus across the disk of the Sun.

Philibert sighed heavily. "Yes sir, if that is your decision, I will certainly comply."

* * *

Philibert made his peace with the decision. Beyond the town and the nearby uplands that had been stripped of their native forests, the wonders of the natural world still thrived. In his time on Ile de France, Poivre had become a student of every aspect of the island. He delighted in sharing his enthusiasm with Philibert.

"Before people inhabited the island," he explained, "Ile de France had been isolated for millions of years. Plant life diversified into untold numbers of endemic species found nowhere else on earth. It was as undefiled as a virgin on her wedding night. There were forests of ebony trees, the largest of them thousands of years old. There were almost no mammals, but birds, and fruit bats proliferated. Wait until you see the monstrous bat creature who lives in the caves. It's a wolf on wings."

"I can't wait to begin," Philibert said.

"I will help get you started. I can show you around the outskirts of town where the wild lands begin. Also, I will put Paul-Philippe de Jossigny, an imminently talented young artist and excellent botanical illustrator, at your disposal. His artistry will make your specimens look like they were picked just yesterday."

Listening to Poivre ignited my imagination, and my enthusiasm for exploration blossomed once again.

On November fifteenth, just one week after docking in port, the fog of uncertainty that clouded our future lifted. Captain Bougainville signed a Certificate of Release, freeing Philibert and I from our duties to the expedition and allowing us to stay on Ile de France as long as we cared to.

It was an enticing prospect, but uncertainty gripped us, not knowing where we would stay. Poivre immediately stepped in and formally asked Philibert and I to stay at Mon Plaisir to assist him in establishing his botanical garden to be named Pamplemousse. He was giving Philibert a chance to be instrumental in the founding of a glorious new botanical garden that would house thousands of species including the spices from the Dutch Indies that they had so jealously protected. It was an extraordinary opportunity.

Not long after we arrived, Monsieur Poivre cordially invited us to dinner. "You must dine with my family. You may bring your servant, and I will bring my wife. She is a truly impressive woman."

At dinner that night Monsieur Poivre elaborated on the history and importance of his plantation. "As a young man, I spent a lot of time in the Far East because my father was a silk trader. I grew up understanding these lands. Everyone knew the Dutch had made a fortune growing spice plants on particular sanctuary islands. They hid them well and the local people were terrified by what would happen to them if they disclosed the secret locations." He paused as a servant refilled the crystal wine glasses. "But I was young, foolish, and full of myself, so I surreptitiously reconnoitered Timor, the Moluccas, and islands off the coast of eastern Africa. At the risk of being discovered, I stole sapling fruit trees, spice plants and seeds. On Timor I found nutmeg plants. At that age, I knew no fear," Monsieur grinned and winked at Philibert. "Or, I should say I knew fear, but to me it felt like excitement. I found one plantation that was not well guarded. Under cover of darkness, I dug up over a thousand plants and brought them back to Ile de France. I have been growing them successfully ever since. I've also collected hundreds of previously undiscovered plants.

I never imagined that I, a simple trader, would have developed such an interest in botany."

"What an astonishing adventure," I broke in. "It is not my place to comment, but I must tell you how inspiring your story is."

Philibert gave me a look that could curdle milk, so I spoke no more.

Poivre looked at me oddly, narrowing his eyes, but turned to address Philibert. "I am now designing a permanent home for them. My days as a trader and adventurer are over. But your reputation precedes you, Monsieur Commerson."

"Oh please, call me Philibert," he demurred. "Your compliment is more than I deserve." But his swelling chest and broad smile belied his false humility.

"It seems quite the opposite to me. Fate has brought you to my shores at precisely the right moment to assist me in my next great project, the creation of a huge botanical garden." Monsieur slapped his open palm on the table, setting the silverware tinkling.

"I would be honored to help. We have had an arduous voyage and assisting you here would be my great pleasure. Very gratifying." Philibert replied with a slight nod of respect.

The opportunity was heaven sent, but one unsolved problem loomed over us. Now that Philibert and I were no longer officially part of the expedition, our pay had been terminated when we were dismissed. All the optimism in the world about the possibilities awaiting us came to nothing if we couldn't afford a suitable place to live.

Though the love affair that started our association was long past, we still functioned well as a powerful botanical team. Together we set off, notebooks in hand, to explore Poivre's gardens. We immersed ourselves in learning all we could about the local flora. It was tempting to simply let practical considerations drift away, but there was a sensitive issue we needed to address with Poivre, and a difficult conversation was unavoidable.

I saw this necessity long before Philibert did, so I confronted him. "You must sit down and have a serious discussion with our host. You must tell him that when we left the ship our income was cut off. He must know."

"I will be humiliated," Philibert objected. "We have enjoyed his gracious hospitality for weeks already. He is feeding us, lodging us, and providing an excellent workspace. How am I going to face the humiliation of confessing our poverty, and admit I can't reimburse him for our expenses?"

"As difficult as it will be, you must. I heard you talking to him about going to Madagascar. Would you expect him to pay all your expenses for such a trip?"

"No, I'm sure he would expect me to cover my own costs."

"Well then, will it be worth some humiliation to participate in that journey?"

"Yes, I suppose you're right."

"You must simply apologize for this misfortune and ask his forbearance. After all, it is no fault of yours that Captain Bougainville decided to go on without you."

"I know what you say is true. I must swallow my pride and admit to Pierre Poivre that, because of my unwarranted dismissal from Bougainville's service, our salaries have been cut off. He needs to know." Philibert parroted my words, making it sound like his idea.

Poivre accepted the explanation with his typical generosity. Shaking his head he shrugged it off. He was far more interested in planning the trip to Madagascar. Philibert met Pierre in his office daily. A peek into the elegant room lined with ebony wainscoting revealed the two men absorbed in conversation. Poivre devised an alternative payment structure that seemed a likely solution.

Poivre wrote a formal letter to the Royal Navy. '*Philibert Commerson and his assistant are diligently pursuing their assigned mission here in Ile de France, conducting important botanical research to enhance the collections at the Royal Gardens, but they are not being paid. And, since Philibert's appointment was made by Royal authority, Captain Bougainville had no authority to override the King's appointment by discharging him on Ile de France.*

I am now providing housing and board, as well as a workspace for Monsieur Commerson. I am therefore requesting reimbursement for food and lodging as well as back payment owed to Commerson's for his salary and that of his assistant.'

It took several months to transmit the message to France and receive a response, but the letter was accurate and convincing, and our payment was forthcoming. We were no longer penniless.

We settled into a comfortable life in a handsome, two-story plantation style home on Poivre's Mon Plaisir estate. The building was surrounded by his seventy-five-acre Pamplemousses Gardens.

"When I bought this property from the previous owner, it had only vegetable gardens," Monsieur Poivre explained. "With dedication and passion, I have turned it into an oasis with hundreds of native species, as well as rare, exotic spices whose value is greater than gold."

His enthusiasm for botanizing was as great as Philibert's, but his knowledge of Ile de France was far greater. The two men developed a sincere friendship sharing their greatest pleasure – botany.

CHAPTER EIGHTEEN

ILE DE FRANCE TO MADAGASCAR
1768 to 1773

Monsieur Poivre made the rounds visiting the elite of French society, introducing Philibert to important local socialites, attending teas and soirees. But the novelty of meeting a new resident soon wore off and the local gentry settled back into their established friendships leaving Philibert to blend into the wallpaper. Instead of trying to insinuate himself into local society, he spent his frenetic energy on a new, all-consuming project. He dedicated himself to developing plans for the improvement of the Ile de France.

For hours he sat at his desk, bathed in tropical breezes that wafted through the tall casement windows, scribbling industriously. He drew remarkably thorough plans for a world-class university he intended to establish. He designed a layout for campus buildings and decided on which men he would install as faculty members to lead the various teaching and research departments. There would be a natural history department, headed by himself, of course. And Veron would lead the mathematics and astronomy departments. He would recruit a respected doctor to anchor the medical studies program. Importantly, the university would have its own printing press to publish the academic treatises the esteemed faculty would compose.

When his enthusiasm for planning fizzled out, we resumed collecting plants with the help of Poivre's young botanical assistant, Paul Jossigny. My meticulous note taking, Jossigny's detailed sketches, and Philibert's choice of areas to explore combined to make these months some of our most productive yet.

There were so many new plants to describe that Philibert began naming them after his late wife, his friends, acquaintances, and supporters. He would sit for hours writing notes about our thousands of finds, while I pressed specimens between sheets of paper designed especially for the task, then labeled and stored them. One day I noticed Philibert and Paul Jossigny laboring to describe a unique plant that seemed to defy the anatomical rules of botany. After they had left the table and wandered off into the gardens, my curiosity prodded me to look at the plant they had been working on. In his notes, Jossigny described it as a tall, shrubby bush which sprouted oblong, egg-shaped, and rounded leaves sometimes all on an individual plant. Scribbled in the description was the genus name, Baretia bonafidia, faithful Baret, with a note: *'Its external garb can be deceptive. It resists a simple description, and cannot be identified at a single glance, as it combines attributes not normally found together in one plant.'* I took a step back, astonished. Should I be flattered that they decided to name a plant after me? No doubt I wore the garb of a man but harbored the soul of a woman. A small smile crossed my lips. Whether they intended it as a description of me or not, they were acknowledging the complexity of my role in their work. I walked away flummoxed but pleased.

Ile de France offered me a freedom I had experienced for only brief intervals since I left La Comelle. The joy of liberty possessed me. I had no need to dread discovery of my sex, no need to fear attack, no need to conceal my knowledge and experience as a botanist. I walked through the town on my own, prowling the back streets, while carefully avoiding the wild, chaotic waterfront. In one pleasant street I found an undeveloped plot of land. It held two small buildings, a garden and a chicken coop. I stood transfixed as visions of my youth in France overcame me. I practically sprinted back to Mon Plaisir. Philibert and Monsieur Poivre sat in the garden deep in conversation. Without a thought for propriety or manners I broke in.

"I have found a lot that's for sale! It's flat, faces the morning sun, and is waiting for a purchaser. It has two small buildings. I could move from the servant's quarters to my own property." The words poured out of me and my face flushed with excitement. Their startled looks silenced me, and I stopped abruptly, not knowing what to say next.

Monsieur Poivre smiled and rose to face me. "Philibert has been telling me about your adventures on the voyage. I understand you better now. I admit I was puzzled when I first met you. It seems you have endured many hardships and took the best possible care of him with your herbal medicines and your diligent ministrations to his wound. He tells me you were also an invaluable assistant in his botanical mission." He turned to Philibert. "Isn't that right, Philibert?"

"Yes indeed, Jean's service has been beyond my highest expectations."

"Now that you have been dismissed from Bougainville's service, have you made a plan for earning your own living?"

I shook my head, completely baffled by this line of questioning.

"In my opinion, you have earned a significant reward, something that cannot be taken away from you, something more than the small salary you earned as an assistant. I will look into the ownership of the plot you mention."

I stared at him in stunned silence, my heart tumbling like rolled dice. Was Monsieur Poivre really that generous? In August 1770, he handed me a land grant letter making me the sole owner of a concession for a block of land on "New Street."

"Here it is, Madame Jeanne Baret, it's yours and no one else's. You are a landowner."

I could hardly believe it. He used my female name. Philibert must have shared the truth with him. This would give me a new measure of independence I'd never known. With title to the land I became a woman of means, successful in my own right. I felt like I should bow down before him or kiss his ring as one would the pope. I was completely dazzled by his largesse. I grasped his hand in both of mine and pumped his arm until he chuckled and gently pulled away. But I had no time to work on the two shacks to make them habitable because we were once again pulled away.

Another adventure beckoned. In October of 1770 Pierre Poivre presented Philibert with a new assignment. We were sitting side by side on a bench in the garden, discussing details about his plant notations, when Monsieur Poivre purposefully strode out to us.

"We have talked about this for months." Monsieur Poivre laid a hand on Philibert's arm. "And today I received this." Poivre extended a clutch of papers toward Philibert.

He fanned through them. The paper was of the highest quality, with the Royal Coat of Arms scrolling across the top of each page. "This looks like an authorization to go to Madagascar." Philibert said, looking up at him.

"Yes, and Jean Baret and Jossigny will go with you." Monsieur Poivre smiled broadly. "This is an official assignment from the French government to conduct botanical research in Madagascar. You and your assistants will all be paid. I wish I could come too, but the responsibilities of my office as Intendente demand that I stay here." He didn't look at all sad, however, as he beamed at Philibert. "I expect you to return with a treasure trove of new knowledge."

"Wonderful!" Philibert bubbled with excitement. "When do we leave?"

"Right away. The ship, the *Ambulante,* is bringing French officials to reinforce our small presence on Madagascar before another country usurps our dominance there. If we want to claim it as French territory, we must have a solid governing presence. You and your assistant will ship out when the ship leaves."

Monsieur Poivre turned to me, smiling. "Pack for a long stay. You will be there on Madagascar for several months at least, perhaps more. I assume, since you have been at his side for such a long time, you are aware of the equipment you will need." I swelled a bit with pride at being acknowledged, but part of me wanted to stay on Ile de France to begin my new life as a landowner and an independent woman. I knew how vulnerable Philibert was without me to tend to him. And the adventure of seeing another barely known island with its new and mysterious plant life was a temptation neither of us could resist. So, I dutifully packed our belongings and equipment, making sure I had paper, plant presses, and a brand-new hand-held magnifying glass Philibert had purchased in Ile de France. My baggy sailor pants and loose linen shirt were brand new and would be the perfect wardrobe.

I was pleasantly surprised to be assigned a private cabin on the *Ambulante*. It was very small, but I had few belongings. It was large enough for a hammock and had a small flat-topped sea chest that doubled as a desk. By this time, most of the people familiar with Philibert and I were aware I was woman, though I still wore men's clothes. A woman traveling on an expedition was not sanctioned perhaps, but no one made an issue of it, and my sex was ignored.

In October, the *Ambulante* deposited us at Fort Dauphin on the southeastern coast of Madagascar. Philibert and I once again tromped around the mystifying island together. While Jossigny joined us occasionally, his attention was often consumed by illustrating the magnificent specimens we brought to him.

It felt odd, like stepping into a fairytale universe, disembarking onto an island with the greatest diversity of species imaginable. The human population was small, mainly French colonists ensconced on their plantations, and African slaves. But the number and strangeness of new species was phenomenal. Monsieur Poivre explained that this island had been isolated for ages, therefore it had given rise to many endemic animals unknown anywhere else on earth. Although our assignment was to find new plant species, we also marveled at peculiar local animal species, like the pygmy hippopotamus, giant chameleon, many types of colorful, curious lemurs, and thousands of plants seen nowhere else. We fell back into the old rhythm of walking the lower elevations together, while I climbed to reach higher places. Despite the wild fluctuations our personal relationship had taken since we met in La Comelle, we recaptured some of the closeness that grows from shared experiences and dreams.

If I thought the lands we explored while crossing the seas were unique and fascinating, Madagascar put them all to shame. We found hundreds of species waiting for us to discover them and share them with the world.

Philibert's enjoyment had dimmed somewhat because of his festering wound and fragile health. But while on Madagascar, his condition deteriorated markedly, and he suffered around-the-clock pain. For many days he spent long hours lying limply on his bed, disabled by gout, and dysentery, and of course his unhealed wound.

"Perhaps we should return to Ile de France," Philibert moaned. We had been on Madagascar a only few months, and had hardly begun our work, but he was already restless, tired, and out of sorts. "It would be delightful to see Pierre Poivre again. Jossigny can continue working on his sketches here, while I dedicate my efforts to writing my account of our circumnavigation and the important scientific discoveries I made."

"That YOU made?" I thought,

I ignored the implication that he had been the only one to discover thousands of new species. It was so typical of him to assume my efforts were subsumed by his.

"Absolutely, I agree. It's time for us to go back to Ile de France."

The *Ambulante* returned to Madagascar's port on its regular route between the islands. We decided that, at our next opportunity, we would board it and returned to Ile de France. Philibert was buoyant, anticipating that, as soon as possible after we reached Ile de France, he would make plans to sail back to France where he would begin work on the mighty botanical tome he planned to publish. He loved to imagine the accolades he would receive. He had always pursued the prize of publication and the notoriety and renown he would enjoy.

This hope triggered an abrupt change of attitude. I had become accustomed to these wild fluctuations of temperament. He immediately became enthusiastic about showing the world his discoveries and their uses. I had my own hopes and dreams for returning to Ile de France. I had my property to return to, my gateway to a new life.

Soon after setting sail, a violent windstorm blew us off course. Though we had endured fierce storms at sea during our voyage, this tempest exceeded the wildest storm I had ever encountered. It forced us to seek refuge on the Ile de Bourbon. News travels fast on an island and before we could disembark the island's chief administrator, Monsieur Cremont, rushed to meet us at the dock. We enjoyed a warm welcome, and he immediately found comfortable accommodation for us. Monsieur Cremont treated Philibert like visiting nobility, strutting around with Philibert on his arm like a valuable ornament, and he set about introducing us to the social elite on his island. Monsieur Cremont's attention flattered Philibert, and the governor ardently promoted the virtues of his island, trying to tempt Philibert into staying longer. Again, Philibert was the center of attention, and he lapped it up like a thirsty dog, as he always did.

Rather than boarding the next ship to Ile de France, he set about enjoying every amenity Ile de Bourbon had to offer. Philibert was so delighted with the company on Ile de Bourbon, that he organized an extended expedition with forty-five people to explore the back country. He gave no thought to his health, or the expense of such an expedition. I took a long breath, exhaled loudly and resigned myself to what turned into an extended stay on this island. I relegated my plans for the future to a far corner of my mind.

There was one adventure on Ile de Bourbon, however, that rivaled all my other experiences. A party put together by Monsieur Cremont undertook a precipitous climb up the Piton de la Fournaise, an active volcano. I could tell Philibert was pushing himself past any reasonable limit of exertion. I was sure he would pay for it later, but in the excitement of the moment, he forced himself forward. Cremont explained that the volcano was active and erupted regularly. We trudged up the black lava rock following our enthusiastic guide. He advised us to cover our noses and distributed kerchiefs to tie around our faces. He harangued us to take only shallow breaths of the sulfurous air. After hours of ascent, we approached the lip of a terrifying crater. It was a vision straight out of hell. The sight of glowing lava, bubbling and seething was otherworldly. Red-orange rivulets slid down the mountain like slow moving infernos, so hot that the sulfurous air itself was on fire.

Our stay on Ile de Bourbon stretched out far longer than I had anticipated. Weeks turned into months until over a year had passed before Philibert once again fell too ill to travel. I felt trapped. My adventure of discovery had turned into a prison sentence. Finally, in January 1772, we boarded the *Ambulante* and returned to Ile de France.

We made our way to Mon Plaisir anticipating a joyous greeting from Monsieur Poivre. But instead of reuniting with our friend, a servant girl we had never seen greeted us at the door.

"I will call the master of the house," she said after we stated our purpose, and she hustled down the corridor. We waited anxiously, mystified by our chilly welcome. Did she say she would summon the master of the house? What did that mean? Where was Monsieur Poivre? We looked at each other completely bewildered. After a lengthy wait, an imposing gentleman with little hair but an abundant girth straining the buttons of his waistcoat came to greet us.

"I understand from my servant that you are Monsieur Commerson. And you are what," he paused, "a botanist?" His voice rose, as if being a botanist was as reputable as being a ditch digger. "I am the new Intendente, Monsieur Maillart. I'm sorry to tell you that Monsieur Poivre has been recalled to France. I have had your belongings packed and stored away. When you find accommodation, you will remove your collections, if that's what you call that assortment of dead plants. Good day, sir." With that, he turned and receded into the airy halls of Mon Plaisir.

Back out in the streets of Port Louis we stared wordlessly at each other. What would we do now? Philibert had spent most of our funds on Ile de Bourbon, indulging his whims for over a year. At one point, he arranged an outing into the back country for fifty people, paying for bearers to transport everyone's belongings, and providing meals for all. It was expensive and foolish, but he was overtaken by one of his overexcited enthusiasms.

Without Pierre Poivre's generosity, we were on our own and had nowhere to go. The first thing we needed was a roof over our heads. I searched the hotels for temporary rooms. There weren't many, and those that were available nearby were shabby, pest-ridden, and noisy. While I searched for a place available immediately, Philibert made the rounds of everyone he still knew in Port Louis, seeking information and advice about longer term housing. I followed every lead, knocking on unknown doors like a poor relative leeching off their goodwill. Landlords were skeptical of Philibert's many crates of botanical specimens and were reluctant to rent to a tenant who had dozens of mysterious boxes emanating unpleasant odors. Our extensive collections contained not only plants, but also fish, birds, insects, and shells. Finding a landlord willing to rent to us for the long term was hopeless. Finally, Philibert scraped together enough money from his friends to put together a down payment on a run-down house in Rue de Pamplemousses. He financed the rest of the cost with a promissory note.

My heart sank when I opened the door to our new house. The memory of the first time I saw our apartment in Paris flashed through my mind. The apartment in Paris was a palace, and I had walked through the doors like a fairy tale princess. This was a tawdry lair. I set to work cleaning and repairing what I could, buying badly used furnishings, and trying to make the inhospitable domicile into a home, however tawdry it seemed.

My concern about Philibert's health deepened into anxiety as I watched him deteriorate. It was as if he had buckled under the weight of his unfulfilled dreams of glory. He now suffered from gout, bouts of bronchitis, pleurisy and the ever-present festering leg wound that would never heal.

One night I found him bent intently over a letter addressed to Fr. Beau, Antoinette's brother, to whom he had entrusted the upbringing of his son, Archambaud. He believed he could still use his inheritance from Antoinette's estate and wanted to claim it. He was grasping at any possibility to pay his debts. It took many months to receive a reply, but when he did, it was not good news. Fr. Beau explained that he had spent the funds for the upkeep of Archambaud, who was now eleven years old.

"For these past nine years I have supplied him with everything he needed, clothing for a growing lad, schooling, food, and a stable homelife. The money was used for the boy."

Philibert, with what little strength he had left, wrote frantically to Naval officers and friends begging them to acknowledge his superhuman efforts and unremitting dedication to accomplishing his botanical mission. He did not enjoy the reception he had dreamed of. He was rebuffed by everyone, sometimes sensitively and sometimes crudely.

"I have been insulted and abandoned," he wailed. They are treating me like a reprobate. They no longer consider me the least bit useful. I anticipated being honored and rewarded for my efforts. I was led to expect respect and renown. Now they have eradicated my salary and rejected any suggestion of compensation. What am I to do?"

I quietly went to his side and placed a comforting hand on his shoulder. Without turning his head, he reached up and covered my hand with his.

"You, at least, have always stood by me. I could always count on your level-headedness, practicality, your fearlessness and your support, not to mention your knowledge of plants."

It was late in coming, but Philibert finally acknowledged his debt to me.

CHAPTER NINETEEN

AFTER THE FALL
1773 to 1774

One day, near the end of February, Philibert concluded that Port Louis, with its fetid atmosphere and clammy humidity, was making his condition worse. He was a man desperately trying to outrun his fate, grasping at any nebulous wisp of hope to fend off his obvious deterioration. He was weak and could hardly breathe, could walk no more than a few meters, his strength sapped by dysentery. But he continued to search for a more suitable environment than Port Louis. He found a sympathetic landlord, Monsieur Bezac, in the Flacq district if the city. Our host, Monsieur Bezac, welcomed us warmly and we moved in.

I packed our plant presses, notebooks, and other collections and arranged for them to be transported to our new location. By the time we arrived at Monsieur Bezac's home, Philibert was so debilitated that, as soon as we arrived, he took to his bed and stayed there. Every day I tended to him as best I could, and each night I kept watch at his bedside. But it was too late. On March thirteenth, his breathing became harsh and irregular, his skin pallid and drained of color. I sat at his side, holding his hand, stroking his forehead until the rasping stopped. He no longer inhabited his ruined body. His skin took on a sickening tinge of grey, his muscles slumped against his bones, and his eyes sunk into their sockets. He was gone. Philibert was buried without ceremony the next day in the Flacq cemetery. It was a lonely death. He had no friends. Monsieur Bezac and I were the only people who watched as Philibert was lowered into his hastily dug grave. I was the only one who lingered, the only one who mourned him.

For all our difficulties, all the vacillations in our relationship over the course of ten years, he was still the most important person in my life. He found me on a rural hillside, a lowly peasant herb woman, and educated me in the skills and methods of botany. He included me on an adventure I could never have imagined, a voyage of discovery that took me nearly around the world. He had been my pupil, my teacher, my lover, and father of my child, and in the end, my inconstant partner. In my way, I loved him despite his faults.

The burial was no sooner over than the reality of my situation began to dawn on me. I was alone with no one in the whole world to help me. I was like a lone seaman marooned on a remote island. No amount of shouting into the wind for help would feed me or shelter me. From this moment I could rely only on myself. For the first time in my life, I could make my decisions without considering the needs of another. My first step was to return to Port Louis. We had amassed a staggering collection of shells, rocks, fish, insects, birds, and as many as six thousand plants. It was up to me to preserve them, catalog them, and protect them. They were our legacy of discovery. I had devoted nearly every waking moment to this task for seven years.

When I arrived at our home in Port Louis, the crossed rifles of French government employees barred my entry. I marched to the new Intendent's offices and demanded an explanation.

"Your activity here was underwritten by the previous Intendente, Monsieur Poivre. He guaranteed the payment on your mortgage and backed your enterprises. I have replaced Poivre, and the French government no longer sanctions your activities. We have been notified that Monsieur Commerson is dead, therefore he will not be making payments on the house. The government has taken ownership of this house and everything in it."

I stood aghast and words would not come. How did they find out so fast? Why would they take action so quickly? He was barely cold in his grave. The guardsmen who barred my entry haughtily turned me away with only the clothes on my back. For a few days, I wandered the streets of Port Louis like a feral dog, deprived of all my senses except the instinct to survive.

For the first time in my turbulent life, I was truly overwhelmed, unable to cope with the calamity I faced, but I couldn't allow myself to sink into helpless despondency. I needed to pick myself up and carry on. As my ability to reason returned, I remembered the lot with its two shabby shacks I had bought before we sailed to Madagascar. Thanks to the generosity of Monsieur Poivre I had no mortgage on the property and the deed was in my name. The thought of starting over yet again gave me a headache. But I would do what was necessary. I found my way back to the shacks, walked in and collapsed with exhaustion. I spread clean, dry rushes on the floor, found a chair, table, a pewter mug, and a rasher from a peddler. As I laid my head down on the balled-up coat that had warmed me in the Strait of Magellan on board the *L'Etoile* and comforted myself with the realization that I had slept just this way in my family home in La Comelle.

The next day, when my head had cleared, I recalled the will Philibert had drawn up before we left Paris. When we lived together on the Rue du Jardin, before the voyage began, Philibert had showed me a copy of the will he had just recorded with the authorities. In it, he granted me all my clothing, the furniture, and permission to live in the Paris apartment for one year if he should die on the voyage. He also bequeathed me 600 livres. One problem remained. I had to find my way back to Paris as soon as possible. To do that, I needed money. I needed to find a job. I had the wages owed to me and a few coins in my waist pouch. I would survive.

I thought of all the usual female employments - laundress, childcare, cook - and I rejected them all. These typically female jobs would never allow me to save enough money to pay for a return ticket to France. The seamen who swarmed the town thought of nothing other than a warm bed and a willing woman, and the oblivion brought by rum and ale. Supplying them with alcohol would be my most reliable opportunity to earn my passage back to France.

As Philibert's servant, I had earned a small salary of twelve livre per month. I had tucked away as much of it as I could. With these small savings I bought women's clothing, bathed, combed my hair and presented myself at La Chapeau Rouge, one of the upscale drinking establishments. I was the ideal employee. I was thirty-three years old, too old to attract male attention, not especially comely, with plenty of experience handling ill-mannered men. I was strong, capable, literate, with basic money-handling skills. They hired me that very day.

I settled into my new life quickly and quietly. The pay was regular, and the work was not burdensome. Unlike many of the business owners in Port Louis, my employer was honest and, as soon as he realized that I could not be fooled about what he paid me, he treated me fairly. Every day, after work, I made my way up the hill to the property I had bought before we left for Madagascar. It was shabby, but I made it as livable as an old shack could be. It would save me the cost of renting quarters closer to the tavern.

I had much in common with the coarse, scruffy sailors who frequented the tavern. We traded stories about the ritual of crossing the line, sometimes exaggerated a bit about the storms we survived, the pirates we evaded, the whales, dolphins, flying fish at which we had marveled. After a few tankards of ale, some of them waxed poetic, describing the boundless canopy of stars under the indescribably black skies, the reflection of the full moon upon a calm sea, the smell of salt air. After recognizing me as a kindred spirit, even though I was a woman, they tipped me generously. My savings grew steadily. Occasionally, some of these men had acquired goods during their voyages and now wanted to trade them for needed cash. Since I still knew many men who had disembarked from the *L'Etoile* with me, I had contacts in town and could arrange trades for my patrons. I earned a tidy fee from each advantageous trade, and with these profits, as well as my wages and tips, my savings mounted.

I slogged through each day, numbed by the shocking turn my life had taken, but I tried not to dwell on it. What good would it do to feel sorry for myself?

Early in 1774, a regiment of soldiers from the Royal Comtois Regiment passed through town on their way back to France. On one mild evening, bathed in a delicate warm breeze, a man wandered into the Chapeau Rouge, sat at the bar and ordered a dark ale. He immediately caught my eye. It was clear from his demeanor that he was not one of the rowdy crowds. He exuded a steady toughness that spoke of a lifetime of worldly experience. He was tall, burly, and a bit stout, no longer young, but still strong. He wore the livery of a noncommissioned officer, complete with tri-corn hat and knee-high white spats. I looked into his comforting eyes, as brown as coffee. My gut clenched as if I might be in danger, and my whole body flushed. I was confused. When we locked eyes, he instantly felt familiar, like someone I'd met somewhere before.

I approached him more tentatively than I did our usual patrons, offering a warm smile – something I never did with the others for fear they would take it as an invitation. His face changed when he returned my gaze as if ten years had suddenly been erased.

"What can I bring you, sir?"

He responded slowly, never breaking his gaze. "I will take a dark ale."

When I place the tankard in front of him, he said "Will you be here tomorrow?"

"Yes, sir. I work here every day except the Sabbath."

"Then I will see you much more often." A sly smile lifted the corner of his mouth. He was staring so intently at me that his tankard missed his mouth, and he dribbled the brew down his chest. I laughed out loud. He was startled and a bit embarrassed, but then started laughing too, as if this was a great joke between the two of us. I felt the earth shift under my feet.

I did indeed see him again. We had friendly conversations whenever he came in. I expected him to ship out and disappear, so I kept a distance between us. After a month or two, we formally introduced ourselves. His name was Jean Dubernat, from the Dordogne region of France. He was true to his word and came to the tavern nearly every night. I was the one who finally broke the ice between us. There weren't many places to meet for a quiet hour or two, but from my days of botanizing, I knew the hidden treasures of the island.

"Have you ever seen the seven cascades?" I asked.

"No, I haven't left the boundaries of the town."

"Let's meet here on my day off and I'll show you around." Pierre followed as I led the way up a lightly used trail through mists cast off from seven cascades. As we climbed, I pointed out colorful plants and birds, and the dramatic view of the coast. The tranquil scene we saw from above belied the unruly town below. Thereafter we found a reason to meet every week.

We shared our stories. Both of us had lived colorful lives, withstanding danger, working arduously, while at the same time honing our skills, mine as a botanist and herbalist, and his as a blacksmith. Our personalities were very different. I was diligent, focused, and strong-willed; he was fearless, mild-mannered, and very funny. I laughed more in one afternoon with Jean and I had in the fourteen years with Philibert. He hailed from a small, quiet town, Saint-Aulaye, in the Dordogne region of France, and I from a small town in Burgundy. We reminisced about our childhoods in our home country.

I thought I had been in love before, but what I felt for Dubernat was like diving into deep water compared to dipping my toes at the shore. He said he felt more relaxed and secure with me than any woman he had ever known. And, yes, we both had our reasons for wanting to return to France.

Our marriage on May seventeenth, 1774, was a quiet affair, attended only by the five witnesses officially required. Our first year together we lived apart, Jean in the regimental barracks and I in my simple shack. Jean petitioned for a position as a Marine, a maritime peacekeeper, on the first ship that needed his services and was returning to France. One year after our marriage, we boarded a frigate and returned to France.

Jean and I used our time on the voyage getting to know each other better, learning each other's peculiarities, foibles, and peeves. It was a joyous time anticipating our life together. But before I left Ile de France, I returned to Philibert's grave in Flacq. I knelt silently in the grass that had overgrown the grave. In another year or two nothing would remain to testify to his burial.

"Dear Philibert. I've come to say my last good-bye. You meant so much to me. Because of you, my life is so much fuller that it ever would have been in La Comelle. You were my world, the father of my son, my teacher, and my mentor. I am leaving now, but you will be with me always."

My feelings were a jumble of rejoicing and regret. It was time for me to leave Ile de France forever, and I was ready.

CHAPTER TWENTY

THE AFTER LIFE
1774 to 1776

The frigate we sailed upon was well-organized, well-provisioned, and manned by professional sailors. The contrast between this crossing and the voyage of *L'Etoile* seven years before could not have been more extreme. The route that took us home was well charted and it took only four months for us to make our way around the Cape of Good Hope, to the south Atlantic, then north along the coast of Africa to France. I gained my sea-legs quickly. Being on the rolling ocean, with the smells of tar and salt air felt almost like home. The first few nights sleeping in my hammock triggered attacks of intense anxiety even though I knew it was irrational and unproductive to relive my past experience. So, one day I made a bundle of my baggy pants, loose shirt, slouchy hat and red sash and tossed it into the sea along with my fears and apprehensions. Those days were over. Because I had no chores or responsibilities onboard, I had time to relax into the rhythm of the ship and allow my memories flow through me. Somewhere near the bulge of the western coast of Africa I began to amuse myself by sketching a very rough map of my route from La Rochelle across the Atlantic, down the eastern coast of South America, through the bleak Straits of Magellan, across the vast Pacific Ocean, over the uncharted waters of the South Pacific, into the winding the labyrinth of islands in southeast Asia, around the Horn of Africa and finally north, back to France.

Looking at the map of my voyage on paper I realized that, when I stepped foot on the soil of my native land, I would be finishing a complete circumnavigation of the globe. A little thrill pushed its way into my heart. Had there ever been another woman to accomplish this feat? It was miraculous. When we landed, there would be no welcoming committee, no representative from the Jardin de Roi, no esteemed scientists to pour accolades on my head as Philibert had envisioned. When Jean Dubernat and I stepped off the boat onto French soil, I had to suppress my impulse to drop to my knees and kiss the ground. Tears filled my eyes. Jean sensed my intense emotional reaction, and he squeezed my hand.

"I understand," he said. "I remember how I felt the first time I returned from an overseas assignment as a Marine. Then, the power of the Regiment directed my life, choose my next assignment, provided structure to my days and planned my future. Even so, when I returned to France, I was overwhelmed with a homesickness I hadn't known I felt. You have had none of that support, my dear." He stopped, with one finger lifting my chin to look at me. His dark eyes calmed me. "But you have me, Jeanne. We will make our way together to my village, Sainte-Aulaye. Have you ever lived in a small, fortified village before?"

"No, my little village nestled into the hills and fields of Burgundy."

His words comforted me. He had felt what I felt now. He understood, and I would not be alone.

"I will give you security you never had."

I rested my head against his broad chest and encircled him with my arms. "Your words soothe me. You are my rock."

Jean smiled, planting a kiss on the top of my head. "I will reclaim my family home and ply my trade. Blacksmithing is an honorable calling. Think of it, Jeanne, you and I living a happy, peaceful life among people who will love you and accept you."

"It is exactly what I have always wanted, a home of my own and a solid future."

I raised my head abruptly and gasped.

"What's wrong? Did I say something wrong?" he said taking a step back.

"I suddenly remembered. Philibert – remember, I told you about him – he willed 600 livres to me. I need to return to Paris to claim it. I am also entitled to the proceeds from the sale of the furniture, and linen from our Paris apartment, and Philibert owed me some unpaid wages. I know how slowly my claim will proceed if I let someone else handle it, so I need to go to Paris and apply for my entitlement myself, directly to the Attorney General in person. As a woman, I cannot expect to be treated fairly. But it will be harder to sweep me under the rug if I am present, demanding what I am owed."

"That's why I love you," Jean said. "You never fail to impress me with your forthright competence. You are a composed, confident, articulate woman and I admire you. I am lucky to have you as my wife."

"I love you too, Jean." I had never expected those words to pass my lips again in my lifetime. But he had burrowed his way into my heart, and it was true. I did love him.

It took some time, but my claim was finally accepted in April 1776. I was awarded 465 livres my 600 livres inheritance. One hundred and thirty-five livres were deducted to cover Philibert's debts. It had been more than a year since Philibert died so I could not take over the lease of the Paris apartment. But I made a small profit from the sale of our Paris furnishings, and I was able to retrieve my clothing. I felt incredibly relieved. A huge burden had been lifted.

* * *

Jean and I settled into a quiet life in Sainte-Aulaye. Memories, both good and bad, replayed themselves in my dreams night after night. Sometimes I awoke laughing and sometimes in a frenzy of terror and fear. Over time, the vividness of the dreams has receded like the bundle of clothing I threw over the ship's rail. I moved on with my life.

One day the entire village buzzed with excitement when a Royal Courier on his richly caparisoned horse paraded down the main street dismounting in front of the smithery.

"I have been told to deliver this letter directly into the hands of Madame Dubernat," he said.

"I am she." I stepped forward and he handed me the document, then turned and rode off as imperiously as he had ridden in.

"What is that?" Jean asked, putting down his hammer. "It has the Royal seal! Is that for you?"

I broke the seal and noted the letterhead of the Ministry of Marine.

Jeanne Barre, by means of a disguise, circumnavigated the globe on one of the vessels commanded by Monsieur de Bougainville. She devoted herself in particular to assisting Monsieur de Commerson, doctor and botanist, and shared with great courage the labours and dangers of this savant. Her behaviour was exemplary, and Monsieur de Bougainville refers to it with all due credit. When Monsieur de Commerson died, this person, whose sex had since been recognized, married one Monsieur Dubernat, formerly a non-commissioned officer in the Royal Comtois Regiment.

Today, Madame Dubernat and her husband, having reached an age that brings infirmities with it and no longer able to earn their living, His Lordship, has been gracious enough to grant this extraordinary woman a pension of two hundred livres a year that shall be drawn from the fund for invalid servicemen.

"This must be the doing of Captain Bougainville," Jean said reading over my shoulder.

"How could that be? He was hardly aware of my existence."

"No, he must have been quite aware of you. You no doubt made a very strong impression on him."

"He could have put me off the ship on any number of occasions, but he did not. He was a good man. He risked his own reputation by allowing me to stay on the ship knowing I was a woman but choosing to ignore it."

The years rolled on peacefully. The countryside, with its rivers flowing through green hills, and verdant forests, reminded me of La Comelle.

In the years since I came home, I have grown old. I have watched a story much bigger than my own play out on the stage of history. I know about the storming of the Bastille, and all the chaos that ensued. I know what happened to Marie Antoinnette and Robespierre. I have seen the rise of Bonaparte. I have even heard the new national song to celebrate our democratic form of government. They call it The Marseillaise. It is a rousing tribute to our nation.

I am sixty-seven years old now and I can see the reaper stalking me from behind every corner. I have outlived everyone I sailed with except Captain Bougainville. All our collections, our notes and descriptions, are protected at the Jardin des Plantes in the Muséum

National d'Histoire Naturelle. The full credit for the collection is given to Philibert, of course, and my existence is ignored, but I take solace in knowing that I have played a part in advancing humanity's knowledge of the natural world.

EPILOGUE

Jeanne Baret and Philibert Commerson collected over six thousand specimens representing more than six thousand species of which three thousand species and one hundred and sixty genera were new to science. By 1773 the collections made their way back to the Royal Museum of Natural History in the Jardin des Plantes in Paris. Even today, collections she carefully dried, preserved, and labeled in her own careful handwriting provide important scientific information.

Over seventy species of plants, animals, insects and mollusks were named Commersonii, a handful were named after Bougainville, and a few after the other officers. Only one species was named after Jeanne Baret. Commerson named it the *Baretia bonafidia,* Good Faithful Baret. But the name did not survive. It had already been renamed by the time Commerson's reports reached Paris. One new South American species in the potato-tomato family, Solanum baretiae, was named in her honor in 2012.

By comparison, Charles Darwin collected one thousand four hundred species of plants during his famous voyage on the HMS Beagle in 1831. Granted, his goal was not to collect only plants, and history credits Darwin's research with concept of the origin of species, but the comparison is still surprising.

Wikipedia tells us that "their collections and papers, gathered in 34 crates embarked on the ship *La Victoire* in November 1773. They bring together seagrass beds from Mauritius, Ile de Bourbon, Madagascar, the Philippines, and include sea coconuts, reptiles, birds, shells, crabs, insects, fish, sponges, and madrepores, lavas, handwritten documents and drawings. All these collections were given to the Jardin du Roi, now the National Museum of Natural History. A large part of the collection has either been lost, never arrived from South America, or was used for the private purposes of other naturalists. Commerson's election to the Académie des Sciences came eight days after his death.

In light of her humble beginnings – born to illiterate and impoverished tenant farmers – Jeanne Baret's accomplishments are almost miraculous. In addition to her scientific contributions, her legacy lies in her strength, courage, ingenuity, and in breaking gender barriers. Though she never sought notoriety and received no recognition for her contributions during her lifetime, she helped destroy preconceived ideas of what women were capable of. Even from a distance of two hundred and fifty years, I hope her accomplishments will inspire women, and others who do not conform to preconceived notions, to break the barriers that constrain them and sail their own voyages.

AFTERWORD

This is a work of fiction. I have made alterations, assumptions, and interpretations that may or may not reflect reality in every detail. I hope those who know far more than I will forgive my errors. My intention was to celebrate Jeanne Baret and be faithful to the spirit and courage she represents.

MAPS

The Jeanne Baret voyage

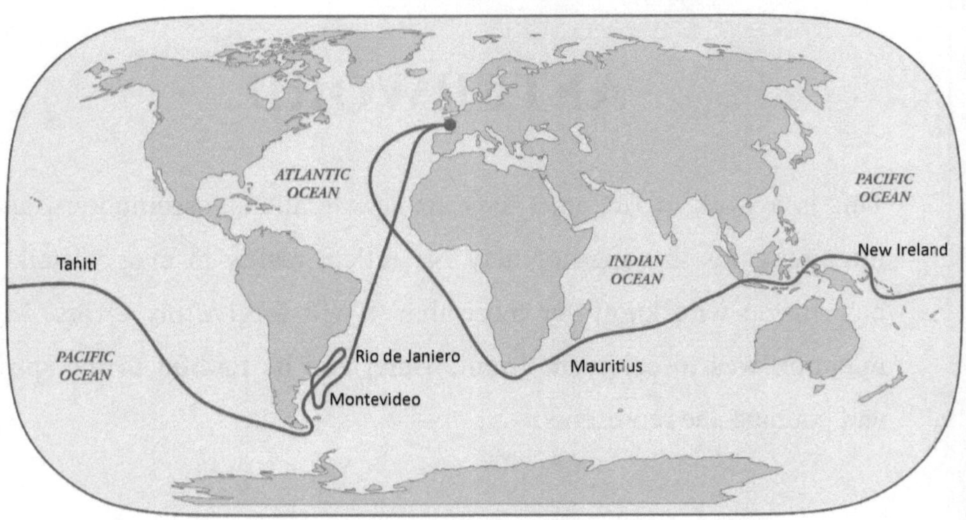

BIBLIOGRAPHY

Bougainville, Louis. *A Voyage Round the World, Performed by Order of His Most Christian Majesty, in the Years 1766-1769*. Cambridge University Press, 2011.

Clode, Danielle. *In Search of Jeanne Barret: The Woman Who Sailed the World*. Danielle Clode, 2020.

Dunmore, John. *Monsieur Baret*. 2002.

Grann, David. *The Wager*. Random House, 2023.

Ridley, Glynis. *The Discovery of Jeanne Baret*. Crown, 2010.

Sides, Hampton. *The Wide Wide Sea*. Vintage, 2024.

ABOUT THE AUTHOR

Cindy Burkart Maynard is passionate about history, and the natural world, a passion that adds rich detail and context to her historical fiction novels. Her characters come to life on the page as they portray what it was like to live in another time and place. She weaves compelling, dramatic stories based on strong characters facing daunting challenges. She has co-authored two nonfiction works about the Colorado Plateau and the Desert Southwest and contributed articles to Images and Colorado Life Magazines. She has been a Volunteer Naturalist for Boulder County for more than twenty years, and served as a Docent at the Sonora Arizona Desert Museum in Tucson, AZ.

Other books by Cindy Burkart Maynard:

"Finding the Way" (The Seekers Series, Book One)

"Esperanza's Way" (The Seekers Series, Book Two)

"Anastasia's Book of Days"

"Soyala: Daughter of the Desert"

Awards:

Colorado Authors League Award Winner for Western literature

Women Writing the West Award Finalist

WILLA Literary Award finalist for soft cover fiction.

Readers' Favorite Five Star Author

Winner of the Marie M. Irvine award for Literary Excellence

Professional Affiliations:

Historical Novel Society of North America

Lighthouse Writers

Women's Fiction Writers Association

Colorado Authors League

Rocky Mountain Fiction Writers

Authors Guild

Follow the author at

www.cindyburkartmaynard.com

www.histoirumpress.com/cindy-burkart-maynard